BELLE

A REGENCY NOVELLA

JENNY HAMBLY

DEDICATION

To Dave,
Thank you for your unwavering support.

CONTENTS

CHAPTER 1

LONDON 1816

Lady Isabella Atherton would have been a most unnatural young lady if she had not been enjoying the heady success of her first season. Her looks alone would always have ensured her a flattering degree of attention; the perfect oval of her face was matched by a flawless creamy complexion and underneath her gleaming golden curls, her quicksilver grey eyes looked upon the world with curiosity and a hint of mischievous laughter. But it was her abundance of natural charm that held the interest of her many friends. She lacked the shyness that hampered so many debutantes and possessed the knack of putting even the most awkward young gentleman or lady at their ease in a matter of moments.

It was true that she had not yet fallen head over heels in love with anyone, but she did not repine. She was enjoying herself hugely and was not at all sure she was yet ready to marry. She knew that some of her friends' mothers were exerting a considerable amount of pressure on them to attract a husband and felt fortunate that her own was not one of them.

Her friend, Miss Lydia Pargeter, was in just such a predicament and so Lady Isabella had agreed to promenade with her in Hyde Park to discuss her options. It was perhaps not the most sensible of places to attempt to hold a private conversation as everyone who was anyone could be found there during the fashionable hour.

"I cannot, I simply cannot marry Lord Banfield, Belle," Lydia said, having to lean in close to prevent the wind whipping her words away before they had any chance of reaching their destination.

"I quite understand." Belle nodded, not quite able to repress a small shiver of revulsion. "I do not like to speak unkindly of anyone, but his teeth are dreadful and his breath quite hideous."

Bright tears suddenly shimmered in the large brown eyes of her friend before catching in her long dark lashes for a moment, like dew hanging from a flower. "But he is very rich, and that is apparently all that is required to make him extremely attractive," she said, sniffing.

"Has he declared himself, yet?" asked Belle.

Lydia shook her head disconsolately. "No, but Mama is certain it is imminent."

Belle's attention was momentarily diverted as she received a nod from a severe looking lady in a passing barouche, who wore an arresting ruby turban, topped with an impressive array of dyed ostrich feathers. She quickly dropped a polite curtsy before turning back to her friend.

Lydia grimaced. "How you can like that old dragon? She makes me quake with fear every time she looks at me!"

Belle laughed. "Oh, she is not so bad. She is godmother to one of my brother's oldest friends. She can be outrageous, I admit, but only because she voices things that everyone else might think but not dare say! I find her quite amusing really."

Lydia did not look convinced. "She would probably say I was fortunate to be courted by Lord Banfield and that it was my duty to accept his proposal, just like Mama."

"If he has not yet asked you, there is no need to despair..." Belle began but was again forced to stop as a young man on a showy but testy mount pulled to a halt beside them, raised his beaver hat, and offered them a small bow. His overlong blond locks and the silk handkerchief he had tied in a rather casual knot around his throat suggested he was of a romantic disposition.

"Good afternoon, Mr Bradford," Belle smiled.

"Lady Isabella, Miss Pargeter," he replied. Although his words addressed both ladies, his eyes drank in every detail of Belle's face as a starving man might view a tempting morsel of food. It seemed he could not look and speak at the same time and as the silence lengthened, Miss Pargeter hastily covered an impolite giggle with a cough.

"Will you be attending Lady Percival's ball?" he finally asked.

Belle took Lydia's arm and pulled her close. "Oh, yes, we will *both* be there, I believe."

"Yes, yes, of course," he said hastily, colouring slightly. "Then I would consider myself the most fortunate of fellows if you would *both* reserve a dance for me."

Before either lady could answer, a high-perched phaeton dashed by at a spanking pace causing Mr Bradford's highly-strung mount to suddenly rear up on its hind legs. Belle and Miss

Pargeter stepped back swiftly, the latter in some alarm, letting out an undignified screech. Mr Bradford, who had only been holding the reins very lightly, would have almost certainly been ignominiously thrown if a large chestnut roan had not suddenly appeared. Its rider took the reins in a firm grip and spoke in a low, soft voice to Mr Bradford's unruly steed. He had the horse back under control in a matter of moments, although the poor animal clearly disliked the crammed avenue and continued to sidle and snort.

"No bottom," the gentleman said laconically, sending Mr Bradford a stern look. "You should know better than to ride such a skittish creature in the park."

Clearly discomposed, Mr Bradford reddened and tried to defend himself, but the gentleman who had saved him from an unthinkable public humiliation had already turned away. There was nothing for him to do but gather the shreds of his dignity and hastily take his leave.

Dismounting surprisingly swiftly for one so large, the gentleman bowed to the ladies.

"Lady Isabella, Miss Pargeter. I hope you have not taken any hurt?"

Lydia shuddered dramatically. "Oh, Lord Hayward, for a moment my life flashed before my eyes. I shall see that fierce beast rearing above me every time I close my eyes."

"Then I suggest you keep them open," he said drily, turning his sleepy blue gaze towards Belle. "And you, Lady Isabella?"

"I do not think we were in any real danger." She smiled. "I would have taken the poor horse's bridle myself if Miss Pargeter had not been clinging to me quite so firmly. It was not his fault, after all."

"Ah, then I can only be grateful that Miss Pargeter had such great presence of mind in a crisis, for it would have been brave but unwise. I take it you do not know what it is to suffer from your nerves, Lady Isabella?"

Belle laughed, not missing the lurking twinkle in those sleepy eyes. "You are quite correct in your assumption, Lord Hayward. But then I have been around horses all my life."

"That would, no doubt, explain it."

"Oh," cried Lydia, "we did not promise Mr Bradford a dance at Lady Percival's ball, after all."

Swinging himself back up into the saddle, Lord Hayward tipped his hat to them. "Then I must stand in his stead. I would be delighted if you both saved one for me."

Not waiting for an answer, he left as unceremoniously as he had arrived.

"Well, I am not at all sure that I will," Lydia pouted, unfurling her parasol as the sun emerged from behind a large grey cloud. "His manners are not quite what I like. He did not even wait to hear our answer, and he was really very rude to Mr Bradford."

Belle chuckled, following Lydia's example and unfurling her own parasol. "Poor Mr Bradford. He is really very sweet."

"Yes," smiled Lydia. "Very sweet on you!"

"Oh, for the moment," Belle agreed. "But he will probably be smitten with someone else by next week. Indeed, I hope he is for although he is charming enough, he has very little conversation! He prefers to gaze, and sigh, and recite the most awful poetry!"

"I would take him over Lord Banfield any day," Lydia said with a heartfelt sigh.

Belle slowed her steps and looked thoughtful as she idly twirled her parasol between her fingers. "Well, he is heir to a viscount, not as good a catch as an earl, I admit, but neither is his fortune to be despised."

"No, but he only has eyes for you," Lydia said a little sulkily. "And anyway, Mama would never consider him when she expects Lord Banfield to declare himself at any moment."

"Even if he does, you need only have a little resolution, Lydia," Belle said a trifle shortly, growing a little tired of her friend's crochets. "You must tell him that you fear you will not suit. No one can make you accept his proposal, after all."

This advice fell on stony ground. "Lord Hayward was right," Lydia complained. "You have no idea what it is like to suffer with your nerves, Belle. If I refuse such an advantageous offer, I will be in deep disgrace! Mother has already declared that I will be whisked back to the country and forced to stay there until I dwindle into an old maid if I do not accept him!"

A fierce gust of wind suddenly whipped Belle's parasol from her hand. Both ladies watched with some dismay as it sailed gracefully through the air for a full two hundred yards before the wind disappeared as swiftly as it had arrived. The parasol dived to the ground with all the purpose of a gannet diving for its prey, the pointed end embedding itself in the grass by the glossy hessian boots of a gentleman neither lady recognised.

This unknown person glanced down at the object for a moment before plucking it from the ground and striding purposefully towards them. Tall and lithe, his claret coloured coat fitted his broad shoulders admirably and his pantaloons displayed his slim, muscular legs to advantage. He paused a few steps from them and removing his hat, offered them an elegant bow, revealing raven black locks that were distinguished by a single streak of white.

"Ladies, please forgive me for approaching you without an introduction, but I fear this is something of an emergency. We must dispense with convention if I am to restore this fine parasol to its owner and thus save her from the dreadful fate of acquiring freckles!"

Lydia giggled, but Belle raised an arched brow. Although she was naturally lively and mischievous, she was also wise enough to realise that she must play by societies rules or be stigmatised as too forward or coming. It was a fine line that she trod with a tripping step.

"It could hardly be called an emergency, sir, when I only had to walk a short distance to retrieve it myself," she said coolly.

His laughing green eyes dropped for a moment to regard the toe of the delicate kid slipper that peeped from beneath her walking dress. "But then your fine slippers would be quite ruined by the damp grass. It was both my pleasure and my duty to save you from such an incon-venience."

Despite herself, Belle's lips twitched in amusement.

Holding out the parasol in both hands as if offering her a rare prize, he bowed again. "The Marquess of Sandford, at your service, ma'am."

Belle inclined her head gracefully. "I am Lady Isabella Atherton, and this is my friend Miss Pargeter."

Lydia curtsied low and peeped up coquet-tishly through her long lashes. "I am pleased to make your acquaintance, Lord Sandford."

Belle took Lydia's arm in quite a firm grip and pulled her close to her side. "We must be on our way, Lord Sandford."

Lydia looked a little disappointed, but she did not demur.

"Might I hope that I have earned a little re-ward, Lady Isabella?" he asked with a roguish smile. "Would you do me the honour of driving with me tomorrow if the weather holds fine?"

"Is not the knowledge that you have done your duty as a gentleman its own reward?" She began to move away.

"Ah, you are like the rest, after all." The marquess sighed dolefully.

Despite her best intentions Belle paused, her

chin raised slightly. "In what way am I like all the rest, sir?"

"You have been warned of my reputation and have not enough spirit to find out for yourself what kind of a man I am."

Belle's eyes glittered. "I have never heard of you before today, and I know nothing of your reputation, sir. Nor do I believe that I have ever been accused of lacking spirit!"

"Prove it." He grinned. "Drive with me tomorrow. You will be quite safe, I assure you."

Never one to decline a challenge, she had agreed quite before she knew it. Satisfied, Lord Sandford bowed low and withdrew.

"Lucky you," sighed Lydia. "He is, perhaps, a little older than I would like but so handsome and a marquess!"

A small frown settled between Belle's eyes. "I am not sure I am lucky at all, for I do not think I should have agreed to it! I know nothing about him after all."

"But that only makes him all the more intriguing," murmured her friend. "I wonder if he will be at Lady Percival's ball?"

He was not. Belle did not know whether she was pleased or disappointed. The season was quite advanced and although she was thoroughly enjoying herself, one did tend to meet the same acquaintances and friends repeatedly. She would have liked to ask her brother, George, Viscount Althorpe about him, but he was at present dancing with Miss Amelia Meliss, a relation of Lady Percival. She sighed. Perhaps it was just as well; it might have been a trifle awkward to explain why she had allowed a complete stranger to approach her. Her brother was handsome, regularly annoying, but always her champion and at times, hopelessly overprotective. Belle stifled a smile as their eyes suddenly met, and she witnessed the barely suppressed boredom which lurked in his eyes.

"Belle," Lydia said. "Wake up, do. Lord Banfield is approaching and I do not wish to dance with him, especially as the next dance is a waltz. What am I to do? Mama will be furious if I refuse."

It was not difficult for Belle to spot Lord Banfield trying to make his way across the crowded room. His figure was portly, his clothing overly ostentatious, and his face rather red. Added to this, he lacked finesse. Rather than clearing a path with a tap on a shoulder or a polite bow and smile, he simply came to a stop or edged himself around the cluster of bodies in a shuffling, awkward, sideways motion.

Feeling a rush of sympathy for her friend, she took Lydia's hand. "Come, we will find a hidden corner until the waltz is over."

Even as she spoke there was a rather undignified scuffle in front of her, as two gentlemen tried to shoulder each other out of the way in an effort to reach her side first. One was Mr Bradford, dressed in a rather flamboyant waistcoat shot through with silver threads, his splendid attire only spoiled by his spindly calves, which the fine silk stockings he wore could not hide. The other was a more restrained looking gentleman, a few years older than his rival, and everything about him was proper and unremarkable.

"I believe this is my dance." Mr Bradford bowed low and stretched out a hopeful hand.

"You are mistaken, my good fellow," the other gentleman asserted in a slightly pompous manner. "I believe I was just before you. Lady Isabella, I would be honoured if you would dance with me."

Belle looked from one to the other in some dismay. "Lord Matcham, Mr Bradford, I am afraid—"

"My dance, I believe."

Belle turned in surprise as the low voice sounded behind her. Lord Hayward bowed over her hand with an elegance not to be expected in such a huge gentleman, his eyes never leaving hers, the lurking twinkle she had noticed before, more pronounced.

She found herself being led onto the floor and cast an apologetic glance over her shoulder in Lydia's direction. She just had time to see Lord Banfield hovering behind her would-be suitors and Lydia grabbing Mr Bradford's hand, all but dragging him into the throng of couples taking their places before the orchestra struck up.

Although Belle had met Lord Hayward a handful of times, she had never seen him waltz. An accomplished dancer herself, she was pleased to find he was light on his feet. Within a matter of moments, they had established a fluid and effortless rhythm.

"Oh, you dance beautifully." Belle smiled brilliantly up at him.

"I think that is supposed to be my line," he said dryly.

Belle laughed. "And why should I not compliment you?"

Lord Hayward did not answer for a moment as he adroitly manoeuvred them around a young couple not as conversant with the dance as they were.

"No reason at all," he said, smiling. "But you meant, I think, that I dance beautifully for a lumbering ox of a man!"

"I will not admit to such a thought," she said primly, even as her eyes laughed.

"I would not expect you to. Your manners are delightful."

Belle dimpled ruefully up at him. "Not on every occasion, I am afraid. I have not yet learned to always think before I speak!"

"Then I hope you will not. At least, not when you are with me."

For some reason Belle felt suddenly bashful. She did not *think* Lord Hayward was flirting with her, but she was not sure. He was older than her other admirers; he must be approaching thirty and had a confidence and quiet way that was not unattractive.

They passed quite close to Lydia and Mr Bradford who were deep in earnest conversation.

"I must thank for you rescuing me from an awkward situation," she said.

His eyes flicked towards the other couple.

"Your thanks might be misplaced. I may have done you a disservice."

Belle looked puzzled. "Oh, in what way?"

"I think that silly young puppy will find a sympathetic ear and a kindred spirit in Miss Pargeter," he said dryly. "I would not be surprised if he transferred his allegiance. Would you mind?"

"Not at all." Belle giggled. "He is quite tiresome, and it may be that he can rescue Miss Pargeter from a..." she hesitated, not wanting to betray her friend's confidence. "A difficult situation."

"I assume you mean Lord Banfield."

Belle looked surprised. Lord Hayward had always given the impression of a being something of a slow top who looked upon the world with a sleepy, disinterested gaze.

"It was not hard to deduce," he said, looking over her head. "That gentleman is behaving in a tiresomely gauche manner for one of his years."

Belle looked enquiringly up at him. He obligingly twirled her about so she could see for herself. Lord Banfield was standing rooted to the spot, following Miss Pargeter's every movement, his eyes simmering with resentment, and his face now more puce than red.

"Oh dear," she murmured, biting her lip. "Her mother will be furious."

"Yes, he is providing a great deal of entertainment for the gossip-mongers and is doing your friend no favours."

Lord Hayward seemed to lose interest in the conversation. "Will you ride with me tomorrow?"

Belle had been contemplating her friend's predicament, but her eyes rose a little bashfully at this unexpected invitation. In other circumstances, she would, she realised, have loved to ride with Lord Hayward.

"Oh, please ask me again another day, for I have already accepted an invitation to go for a drive with Lord Sandford."

"Is that wise?" he said quietly, his gaze enigmatic.

"I am not sure," Belle admitted frankly. "He told me he had something of a reputation and challenged me to drive with him anyway."

"Ah, I see. I suspect you are not a lady who easily backs down from a challenge."

Belle's smile was again rueful. "No. Is he so bad?"

Lord Hayward considered this question thoughtfully. "He has always been a little wild and is more often under the hatches than not. You will no doubt find him amusing; he has a way with the ladies and has left a few broken hearts in his wake over the years."

The music came to an end.

"Thank you for the warning and the dance." Belle smiled, offering him a graceful curtsy.

Lord Hayward took her hand and bowed over it. "I have rarely enjoyed a dance more," he said, giving her a searching look. "If you find yourself in need of any further advice, on any matter, you will find me very discrete."

As he disappeared back into the crowd, Belle stood looking thoughtfully after him for a few moments, surprised at how comfortable she had felt in his company.

CHAPTER 2

"Thank you, Radcliffe." Belle dimpled as the butler placed a silver tray generously laden with cards, letters, and posies of varying colours on the breakfast table beside her.

"They really are tipping the butter boat over you, aren't they?" said her brother, just then entering the room and casting a jaundiced eye in her direction.

"Not at all, George," his mother, Lady Atherton said calmly enough, but with a quelling glance in his direction. "Belle is merely receiving her due as this season's most sought after debutante."

He ejected a harsh crack of laughter. "Must be all about in the head, the lot of them! A young lady is meant to be meek, obedient, and docile!"

"Says who?" Belle pouted, her eyes alight with challenge.

"James Fordyce," George replied, adding a slim volume to her tray. "I found it in the library yesterday."

"Sermons to Young Women." Belle read the title with such loathing in her voice that her brother grinned despite himself.

"Oh, you, you…" Not managing to immediately find an epithet that did justice to her feelings, Belle was reduced to schoolroom tactics. She hurled the book down the table in his general direction just as he was seating himself. He caught it deftly in his left hand, even as he reached for the coffee with his right.

"Belle!" Lady Atherton said sternly. "Whilst I acknowledge that George is being quite unnecessarily provoking, I will not have you behaving in such a hoydenish manner, especially at the breakfast table! If you do not cease immediately, you will read that book from cover to cover!"

Three pairs of almost identical silver-grey eyes observed each other assessingly for a moment before a mischievous twinkle crept into them all and they smiled simultaneously. The likeness between them was clear, although

George possessed thick, curling, chestnut hair, whilst Belle and Lady Atherton were both fair.

"I'm sorry, Belle," her brother said wryly. "I am sure you deserve every attention bestowed upon you. Thank God you are not meek and docile!"

Belle looked thoughtful for a moment as she sifted his words for hidden meaning, then quirked an amused brow. "I take it Miss Amelia Meliss did not capture your interest, then?"

She let out a tinkle of laughter at the look of revulsion that momentarily marred her brother's handsome features.

"Couldn't get a word of sense out of her," he admitted. "Her undoubted beauty is only matched by her lack of sense. She had not an original thought in her pretty head. Why I agreed to escort you and Mama to all these infernal squeezes is beyond me!"

Lady Atherton smiled fondly at him. "It is because you are a very good son and brother. You know your father would be made miserable if he came to town." She cocked her still pretty head to one side and regarded the rather fine timepiece sitting on the mantle over the fire a little pensively. "Although you are a little crotchety before midday."

Belle had begun sifting through her mail and suddenly began to giggle.

"Let's hear it," said her brother, with a marked lack of enthusiasm.

Belle cleared her throat and tried to look serious as she began to read.

'Your smile is like the sun,
Your eyes like stars that shine,
Please say that I'm the one,
That may claim your heart as mine!'

"Oh dear," murmured Lady Atherton.

"I wish I hadn't asked," groaned George. "It's almost enough to put a man off his food. Who is it? Matcham or Bradford?"

"Bradford," acknowledged Belle. "He really is very sweet, but frightfully dull. This is from Matcham," she said, picking up a single pink damask rose. "*Wear this for me that I may hope…*"

George quirked an enquiring brow. "And will you give him hope?"

Belle smiled. "I am not so cruel. Besides, I have agreed to drive in the park with the Marquess of Sandford. I am set on wearing my new blue spencer and as I never think blue and pink go well together, I cannot!"

"Sandford?" he frowned. "I had not realised he was in town or that you had been introduced to him."

Belle shrugged carelessly, but a slight pink tinge crept into her cheeks. "I met him in the park yesterday."

"And who introduced you?" George persisted.

"Oh, I don't know," Belle blustered, unwilling to reveal to her suddenly prosy brother that he had introduced himself. "There were so many people out."

"I am not surprised," said Lady Atherton. "I have never known such a cold, wet June. It is such a relief to see the sun again, even if there is still a nasty, cold wind blowing."

When Belle left the room, George turned to his mother. "Do you really intend to let her go with Sandford?"

Lady Atherton met his eyes steadily. "I would rather she did not," she admitted. "His title does not alter the fact that he is too old for her, not to mention too cynical, and if rumour is to be believed, something of a rake!"

"Then why allow it?" George pressed.

"Are you trying to tell me how to manage my daughter, George?" He did not miss the thread of steel that wound through the soft utterance. "Sullied though his reputation may be, Sandford is still accepted everywhere and so I can hardly forbid Belle to acknowledge his acquaintance. As he has unfortunately decided to come to town, she was bound to meet him eventually, and I think you will find that the object that is forbidden becomes instantly more attractive. Belle may have a natural liveliness, but she has been reared with good principles, we must take some comfort in that."

A wry smile twisted his lips. "I'm sorry, Mama," he said gently. "You are, of course, correct. It is just that Belle is a little out of the ordinary and ripe for mischief. I find it very hard to imagine that she is likely to become enamoured with any of her current swains. They are admittedly many, but also dreadfully dull. I was amazed she saved a waltz for Hayward last night; they don't come more staid than him!"

Lady Atherton thought this over for a moment. "I would say dependable rather than staid. He may not be dashing, but he has a pleasing countenance. He could have picked any number of eligible young ladies the last few seasons, but as he has not, I think there might be more to him than meets the eye."

"If you say so," George replied, sounding unconvinced. The image of his childhood friend, Philip Bray, swept into his mind. Captain of a Hussar regiment, he might have been the very man for her. "It is a shame Philip has not yet returned from France; he is the only man I know who might be able to keep her in check."

Lady Atherton smiled. "Perhaps, but I think that he still regards Belle as a child, and he spent so much time with us growing up that I fear she regards him more as another annoying brother! Besides, now Wellington has decided the art works Bonaparte plundered from across Europe and added to the Louvre's collection must be returned to their rightful owners, I hear there is much unrest in France, so I think he will not return for a while yet."

George nodded his assent. "I hear Prinny expressed an interest in acquiring a few, but his hopes have been dashed by Liverpool as we can hardly claim that we are impartial if we allow him to accept any. I hear a few valuable paintings have gone missing on their way home."

Lady Atherton shrugged. "Yes, it is unfortunate, but the world has always had its share of ruthless opportunists."

"Let us hope that Sandford will not prove to be one of them!" growled her son.

Belle dressed with care for her appointment with the marquess, donning a high dress of jaconet muslin, its simplicity offset by a close-fitting spencer in sapphire blue. Set atop her golden curls was a white chip hat lined with white satin. Its small front offered some shade without obstructing the view of the wearer, and a low plume of white feathers tipped with blue added distinction to its moderate crown.

"Very fetching, dear," approved Lady Atherton, who Belle found waiting in the hallway as she ran lightly down the stairs. "Although perhaps a pelisse might offer you more protection from the chill wind?"

"Oh, please do not fuss, Mama, I will be perfectly comfortable." She kissed her quickly on the cheek before walking out of the front door, which the footman was holding open.

Lady Atherton followed her and inclined her head coolly in response to the Marquess of Sandford's bow.

"Lord Sandford," she said, giving him a steady look. "I hope you have a blanket in your carriage and will not keep Lady Isabella out too long, for this wind is quite cutting."

"You can be sure I will take every care of her, ma'am," he returned.

"See that you do."

"I fear your mama does not approve of me," he said when they were out of sight of the house, the lurking twinkle in his eyes at odds with his rueful tone. "Her look was quite as cutting as the wind."

"Is there any reason she should approve of you?"

The marquess let out a harsh laugh. "No, none at all. How did you persuade her to allow you to drive with me?"

Belle looked archly at him. "No persuasion was necessary."

Lord Sandford smiled crookedly. "Then Lady Atherton is either very wise or very foolish."

"I believe my mother trusts me to conduct myself well in *any* company, even yours."

He looked amused. "So, the kitten has claws!"

"Well, your reputation precedes you, after all." She grinned up at him.

He looked down at her for a long moment, his green eyes intent. "And what have you discovered about my reputation?"

Belle coloured as she realised she had revealed that she had been making enquiries about him. She shrugged. "Oh, nothing much, you are perhaps known for being a trifle wild. But we agreed, did we not, that I must decide for myself?"

Lord Sandford gave a harsh bark of laughter. "Any man who has not been caught by the parson's mousetrap by my age, must either be seen as a rake or a damned dull dog!"

Although it was not at all the thing to use such language in front of a lady, Belle was too used to hearing the epithet on the lips of her brother or father when they were enraged, to pay it any notice.

"Talking of dull dogs," he murmured as he turned neatly into the park, "here comes Hayward."

Belle felt herself bristling at his sneering tone. "Lord Hayward is a friend of mine."

The marquess quirked an ironic brow in her direction. "Is he now? No wonder you agreed to drive with me. If that is the stamp of your admirers, you must be bored to death, poor girl."

Belle coloured and turned away from him. She noticed Lord Hayward was riding a different horse, and she just had time to admire the handsome chestnut stallion and its rider's fine seat before he came up beside them.

"Lady Isabella, Sandford," he said, tipping his hat to them.

"Hayward," the marquess replied, his eyes roaming over the fine mount. "So, it was you who bought Sir Gareth Bray's stallion at Tattersalls last week. Paid a hefty price, I hear."

Lord Hayward looked at him from beneath sleepy lids. "Quality is always worth paying for."

"He is handsome, everything prime about him," said Belle, suddenly wishing she had agreed to ride with Lord Hayward; she was not enjoying Lord Sandford's company as much as she had expected to.

"Indeed," agreed the marquess, "would have been interested myself if I had had the blunt."

Lord Hayward looked bored. His glance strayed to the showy pair that pulled Lord Sandford's curricle. "I see you picked up Chandlomey's breakdowns instead."

The marquess's eyes narrowed. "There's nothing wrong with this pair, Hayward."

"All show and no go," Lord Hayward drawled.

Belle gasped, it seemed the usually placid Lord Hayward was intentionally provoking the marquess. The red bar of colour that slashed across his cheekbones and the glitter in his narrowed green eyes, suggested he was succeeding.

"I'd back them against anything you have in your stables,' he said from between gritted teeth.

"How very rash of you," Lord Hayward said softly. "When you have no idea what sort of cattle I keep."

"I don't need to," the marquess snapped. "I

will own myself astounded if you have ever par-taken in a race on the public roads before."

Belle found herself holding her breath, both repelled and intrigued by the tension that arced between the two gentlemen.

"I have not," agreed Lord Hayward. "Unlike you. Your reckless races used to be legendary. But then, just because one does not choose to flaunt one's skill, it does not necessarily follow that one does not possess it."

"Name the stake, day, time, and place, Hay-ward. If you are so set on making yourself a laughing stock, who am I to stop you?"

Lord Hayward named a sum that made Belle's jaw drop. The marquess might have indi-cated that he was not very flush in the pocket, but he accepted the two thousand pound stake without a blink. The race was to occur two days hence; they would start at Islington, cross Finchley Common, pass through Barnet, and finish at Hatfield.

Once the details had been agreed, Lord Hayward turned to Belle. "Lady Isabella, would you care to ride with me tomorrow?"

"Yes," she said, gathering her scattered thoughts. "I love to ride. It is a shame we cannot gallop in the park."

He gave her a sleepy grin. "It is entirely possible, ma'am. You must, however, be prepared to leave early, before breakfast would be the best time."

Lord Sandford let out a crack of laughter. Belle ignored him, her eyes sparkling with anticipation. "I will be ready."

"Until tomorrow, then," he said, bowing his head to her.

It had been a most extraordinary encounter, and Belle did not know quite what to make of it. She cast a wary sideways glance in the direction of her companion. His bad humour had gone, and although his eyes still glittered, it was with the feverish anticipation of the gambler.

As the marquess skilfully wove his way amongst the traffic, he let out a low chuckle.

Belle's brows rose. "It is a fortunate man indeed, who can laugh at the prospect of losing such a large sum of money."

Lord Sandford looked down at her, his face full of mockery. "Do not worry your pretty little head on my account, Lady Isabella, there is no such prospect; it will be the easiest money I have ever earned! And I have you to thank for it! I knew there was something about you that would bring me luck."

Belle looked nonplussed. "What has all this got to do with me?"

Lord Sandford's laugh was edged with scorn. "It has everything to do with you. Only a man deeply in love would go against his character in such a way! If I am not much mistaken, Hayward does not think me worthy of your company, and he thinks to punish me for my presumption or impress you. Either way, he is a fool and a dullard. It is he who is unworthy to aspire to the heart of someone as bright and spirited as you."

The compliment fell on deaf ears. "Lord Hayward is not my suitor. He has never tried to woo me," Belle said quietly.

"Putting himself up for such public scrutiny and humiliation is not the usual way to woo a lady, I admit, but then, did I not just say that he is a fool?"

Belle frowned, feeling increasingly uncomfortable in his company. "Public scrutiny?"

The marquess nodded, his attention on the road. "The bet will be entered in the book at our club," he explained.

Belle shivered and pulled the blanket closer around her as the wind gusted across the park.

"Is that not another of your friends ahead?"

Glad of the change of subject, Belle followed his gaze and saw Lydia bowling towards them in a high perch phaeton. She looked both miserable and terrified as she clutched the side of the high, swaying body of the equipage. Lord Banfield sat beside her. He appeared fully occupied trying to control the beautiful high-steppers that pulled it.

The marquess gave another low chuckle. "Miss Pargeter has every reason to feel afraid," he said. "Banfield's love of display is unfortunately not matched by any great ability, in fact, he is completely cow-handed!"

Belle was growing tired of his constant sniping at the expense of others. She saw Lydia say something to her escort and point in their direction. Lord Banfield acknowledged Belle with a brief nod, but as his glance rested on the marquess, he frowned and urged his horses onwards. Lydia turned as they passed and sent Belle a tearful look.

"Miss Pargeter could not look more miserable if she were on her way to the gallows," Lord Sandford commented. "Do not tell me she is going to marry that great tub of lard?"

"I hardly know," said Belle, unwilling to fuel his malicious humour. She had been surprised that Lord Banfield had failed to stop when Lydia had so obviously made her wishes clear, and now became conscious of the curious looks they were attracting from various passersby.

"How bad is your reputation?" she said uneasily.

The marquess grinned unrepentantly down at her. "Not so bad that I am persona non grata, not so good that matchmaking mama's throw their daughters at my head! Do you really care so much for public opinion?"

"Not overly," Belle replied with a touch of bravado.

"Prove it!" he pressed. "Come with me to a masquerade at Vauxhall. You will enjoy it vastly, I assure you. It is far more amusing than the usual round of insipid balls."

For a moment, Belle's eyes lit up. "Do you mean to get up a party? I would like to see the fireworks, I must confess. I have heard that there is a lady who walks out of them on a tight rope!"

The marquess smiled at her enthusiasm, and Belle reflected how much more handsome he was when he wasn't mocking others. "Madame Saqui. I saw her perform in Paris. She is remarkable. But I will not be arranging a party, that would be dull, and I am never dull! We will have much more fun on our own, you know."

Belle's eyes widened in shock.

The mockery was back in Lord Sandford's eyes. "Come, come, child. Where is all that spirit now?"

Belle was not fool enough to be caught in the same trap twice. Her eyes flashed with all the spirit the marquess could wish for. "Do not mistake having some delicacy of principle with a lack of spirit, sir. You have no reputation left to lose it would seem; the risk would be all on my side. It is the sort of bad bargain you appear to enjoy! You have misjudged me if you think a wish for a little excitement would lead me to behave in such a rash and potentially damaging manner. I only hope you have also misjudged Lord Hayward, and that he will succeed in punishing your presumption!"

A slightly ugly look distorted Lord Sandford's features. Belle was relieved to hear a voice hailing her from an approaching carriage. A very handsome lady in a vivid blue turban pulled up beside them. She looked at the marquess with some disdain.

"Sandford," she barked in a low, gruff voice. "Decided to drag your good-for-nothing self to town, eh?"

Belle was surprised to see a glimmer of amusement lighten his eyes.

"Lady Renfrew, it is always, er, refreshing to see you."

"Palaverer,' she snapped, but Belle thought she saw a gleam of appreciation in her slate-grey eyes. "I am not one to begrudge any man his diversions, but you will not amuse yourself with any young friend of mine."

Her tone brooked no argument. She turned to her companion, a very well dressed if rather plump man, with twinkling conker brown eyes. "Get down, do, Percy. I will take Lady Isabella home. She looks quite frozen."

The gentleman did her bidding without fuss and helped Belle down with an old fashioned gallantry. Belle knew Sir Percy Broadhurst and smiled gratefully at him.

"Give me a lift will you, Sandford?" he said, heaving himself up into the space she had just vacated.

"Hrmpf! The walk would do you good, Percy. You are becoming fat as a faun!"

Lord Sandford let out a bark of genuine laugher drawing Lady Renfrew's fire again.

"As for you, sir, find your amusement with someone who is up to the mark and knows how to play the game!" She nodded imperiously at her driver and waited until they were out of earshot before turning to Belle.

"He is an amusing rattle, my dear, but not to be trusted in the least. I do not know what your mother was thinking of to allow you to be seen driving with him. I shall certainly have a word in her ear!"

Belle had a natural empathy towards her acquaintances that once engaged, enabled her to do or say just the thing that would ensure their goodwill towards her. It was not a calculated thing, but more of an unconscious tap into their true personality rather than the front they put on for the benefit of society. So rather than quaking in her boots, as Lydia and many others would have surely done in her place, she reached out and took Lady Renfrew's hand in her own.

"Thank you, dear Lady Renfrew. I was beginning to feel excessively uncomfortable in Lord Sandford's company, and am really very grateful to you for taking me up."

"Hrmpf! Tried to persuade you to get into some sort of mischief, I'm sure. Well, if you put him in his place, and the sour look on his face when I rolled up, would suggest that you did, I can only say that you have more sense than I ever gave you credit for!"

Rather than take offence, Belle laughed. "But not enough sense to refuse an invitation from a stranger who told me he had a reputation in the first place!"

Lady Renfrew let at a low crack of laughter

and patted Belle's hand. "Used that as his bait, did he? Well, it is hardly surprising it worked! You have spirit, gal! And I like you all the more for it, but take care it doesn't lead you into trouble. It is a shame that town is full of fools at the moment, but there it is, you'll have to make the best of it."

CHAPTER 3

Belle was glad to spend a rare night at home with her mother; she had a lot to mull over and an early morning ahead. Lady Renfrew had indeed had a short private interview with Lady Atherton on their return, and Belle had awaited the results with some trepidation. But other than complimenting her on gaining that redoubtable lady's good opinion, her mother had not given her the grilling she had half expected. She felt sure George would not have let her off the hook quite so easily, but as he had taken the opportunity to escape for an evening with his cronies, she did not even have to run the gauntlet of his probing questions.

She sat idly flicking through the pages of The Lady's Monthly Museum, her brow slightly furrowed, as she tried to hit upon a way to persuade her mother that a ride before breakfast with a gentleman was perfectly acceptable.

"Bother!"

Belle glanced over at Lady Atherton, who was sucking on the pad of one delicate finger, her sewing abandoned on the occasional table beside her. She smiled gently across at her daughter. "How very careless of me! It would seem that both our minds are elsewhere."

"Elsewhere?"

Lady Atherton raised one brow and gave her daughter a dry look. "Well, unless you have suddenly developed the ability to read with amazing speed, that is. Out with it, dear, am I really such a dragon that you cannot simply tell me what is on your mind rather than cast about for the best way to do it?"

Belle's brow cleared and she grinned. "You are never a dragon, Mama! It is just that I have made an arrangement I am not sure you will like, and I am so looking forward to it."

Lady Atherton looked a little startled but said calmly enough, "*Not* with Lord Sandford?"

"No," Belle assured her. "I drove out with him out of curiosity, you understand."

"Of course," her mother replied, her tone very matter-of-fact. "Once you had met, it was inevitable. And has your curiosity been satisfied?"

"Yes. *He* tried to make an arrangement I *am* sure you would not like, but do not worry; I turned him down."

"Oh?" Lady Atherton prompted.

"He wanted to take me to Vauxhall Gardens." She could not help sounding a little wistful. "I have always wanted to go, you know."

Lady Atherton looked thoughtful. "It is not what it once was, Belle. It used to be quite unexceptional, but standards have fallen in recent years. Still, if he had arranged a respectable party, we might have considered it."

Belle dimpled. "But that would be dull, Mama, and the marquess of Sandford is *never* dull!"

Lady Atherton rolled her eyes. "I can almost hear him saying it. I suppose his proposal was of quite a different nature, then?"

Again Belle grinned. "Indeed. He wanted to escort me to a masquerade, *alone*."

"How very shocking!" Her mother smiled. "And how exciting!"

Belle blinked in surprise. Her mother had always had her own ways of managing the various characters in her family, and shock and outrage had never been amongst them, even so, she had not expected her to take her revelation quite so calmly.

Lady Atherton's face softened, and a dreamy look shimmered in her silvery eyes. "I was young once, you know, and I was no mean bit if I say so myself."

Belle laughed. "You are still a beautiful woman, Mama. I am sure you had lots of admirers! Tell me all about them!"

Lady Atherton shook her head gently as if in doing so, she could shake off a lingering memory. "Not tonight, dear. Now, tell me about the arrangement you are *not* sure I will approve of."

After her recent revelations, an early ride with Lord Hayward, accompanied by her groom, of course, seemed quite tame and her mother capitulated with remarkable ease.

"It is perhaps not usual, but I cannot see the harm. I know how much you miss your rides, my dear. Consider it a reward for behaving so well with the marquess, not that I would expect anything less of you. And anyway, you will be quite safe with Lord Hayward, of that I am certain."

"Yes, that is just what I feel, Mama."

Belle retired early to bed and fell asleep almost immediately. She was deep in vivid dreams – one moment being whirled around an outdoor dance floor by a mysterious stranger in a mask, and the next being jolted until her teeth rattled in her head as Lord Hayward cracked his whip and urged his team to catch Lord Sandford's – when her maid woke her. It took her a moment to realise where she was.

"Is it morning already, Sheldon?" she yawned.

"Barely, ma'am," the maid replied a little sulkily.

"Oh, don't look so Friday faced, Sheldon! You had every opportunity for an early night." Belle jumped out of bed and crossed to the window. "Now, if only it is not raining!" She pulled back the curtain to a drab but dry, grey sky.

"I will match the weather. My grey habit, I think!"

Belle's riding habit may have been grey, but it was anything but drab. It was made of a fine, slate-coloured cloth, with the body short in the waist, and it was braided in a very rich manner. She matched it with a severe, tall crowned hat of a similar colour, free of any adornment. Indeed, it was unnecessary, as her golden curls clustered under the brim quite charmingly, the dark colour of the ensemble ensuring her burnished locks glowed warmly in contrast.

Both her groom, Hobbs, and Lord Hayward were waiting when she emerged from the house.

Handing the reins of his own mount to Hobbs, Lord Hayward strode forwards to toss her up into the saddle himself.

"I do hope I have not kept you long, Lord Hayward," she said, smiling down at him as she settled herself and patted the neck of her dapple-grey mare.

"Not long at all," he confirmed. "Your promptitude does you great credit, ma'am. It is not something I always associate with the females of my acquaintance."

Belle gave him an impish grin. "Well, it was no hardship, sir. I often ride before breakfast when we are at Atherton. I have a restless nature you see, and must always be doing something!"

He gave her his sleepy smile as he swung up into the saddle. "You ladies are all so accomplished."

Although the hour was early, the streets were already alive with carts and drays carrying a variety of produce to market. Street vendors selling anything from oil or salt to fruit and flowers called out their wares. Bakers' boys, carrying great loaves of bread on wooden trays hurried between pedlars with cakes or maids carrying heavy buckets brimful with milk.

Belle wrinkled her nose as she considered his words, before saying with characteristic frankness, "I am afraid I must fall short if we are to compare my accomplishments to those of other ladies. I have never been able to sit still long enough to excel at sewing or drawing. I can play the pianoforte in a passable fashion, sing a little, dance and ride, but I am afraid that is the sum of my achievements!"

Lord Hayward nodded. "But then, all these accomplishments do not carry equal weight."

Belle quirked an enquiring brow. "They don't?"

"No," he said decisively, his voice grave. "I have a drawer stuffed full of tributes from a well-meaning aunt who appears to think I am constantly in need of slippers or embroidered handkerchiefs!"

Belle laughed. "You are fortunate to have such a kind aunt who clearly holds you in high regard."

"Perhaps," Lord Hayward said. "But I would much prefer a lady who could please my ears with a song, or dance without stepping on my toes!"

A cart carrying barrels of mackerel passed rather close to Belle's mount, causing the mare to shake her head and sidle. Lord Hayward automatically reached out a hand, but Belle had her back under control in a moment. "Come now, Hebe," she said gently, "this is no way to behave in company."

Lord Hayward smiled and added, "Or accompany me on a ride without me having to worry about her taking a tumble every time her horse took a fence or objected to a passing carriage."

Belle felt warmth suffuse her cheeks at his gentle compliments and was glad when they turned into the park. She was unsure how seriously to take them or how to effectively parry them without giving offence. In short, she felt a little out of her depth. Seeing the long, largely empty ride in front of them, she suddenly urged Hebe to a canter and then allowed her to lengthen her stride into a gallop.

Lord Hayward's handsome stallion easily matched her. They rode for some time, only the sound of hooves thundering on the ground and bird song breaking the silence. When they pulled up, her eyes were sparkling and her cheeks flushed from the exercise.

"Thank you, Lord Hayward. I cannot remember when I have enjoyed myself more!"

"Ah, do not tell me you have joined the ranks of jaded ladies who find all the myriad entertainments of the season a sad bore."

"Not at all," Belle assured him as they

turned their mounts and continued back down the avenue at a sedate trot. "I am enjoying myself hugely, but our early ride has the advantage of novelty."

"And did not your outing with Lord Sandford also have the merit of novelty?"

Belle coloured and her eyes flew up to meet Lord Hayward's suddenly intent gaze. "You are to race him tomorrow! I had forgotten."

"It is of no moment," he said quietly.

"But why did you challenge him?" she asked curiously, still unable to credit the idea that she was the cause.

Lord Hayward gave a careless shrug. "Perhaps, that too, has the advantage of novelty."

Belle turned this over in her mind for a moment before nodding and smiling brightly at him. "Of course, and why shouldn't you have a little adventure? I only hope you beat him soundly!"

It appeared that news of the forthcoming race had spread like wildfire. George was full of it at the breakfast table.

"I cannot think what can have possessed him! Who would have thought Hayward had such bottom?"

Belle felt herself bristling in his defence. "I have not noticed that Lord Hayward lacks bottom. Do not all gentlemen enjoy the odd adventure?"

George regarded his sister incredulously for a moment. "Not all, Belle, no. And I have never heard the words Hayward and adventure mentioned in the same breath before."

"But then, how well do you know him, after all?"

"He is not in my close circle, I admit. But I think you will find that general opinion is on my side. They are offering very long odds on him."

"Well, I think he will do very well," she asserted firmly. "In fact, I would like you to place a bet on him for me, George."

Her brother's mouth dropped open.

"Now, Belle, it is not at all the thing for young ladies to bet on such affairs," Lady Atherton said reprovingly, watching her daughter closely over the rim of her teacup.

"No, and I won't do it!" exclaimed her brother. "I am sorry if you think me disobliging, Belle, but it won't do."

"Well, I do find you disobliging. I am becoming heartily tired of all the restrictions placed on 'young ladies'. It is all so dull." She hunched a rather sulky shoulder in his direction and very soon became absorbed in a letter that had been placed by her breakfast plate.

Her brother cast a wary eye in her direction. "Yesterday, you went for a drive with Sandford, and today it was an early morning ride with Hayward. It seems to me you are already testing those restrictions to the limit, Belle. What will be next?"

Belle folded the letter she had now finished perusing and slipped it into her reticule, a thoughtful expression dulling her usually expressive eyes.

"I refused an invitation from Lord Sandford to take me to a masquerade at Vauxhall," she said quietly, her head tipped to one side as she regarded her brother, her expression angelic.

George choked on his coffee. "That damned rascal!"

"George!" Lady Atherton spoke sharply, and a dull colour suffused his high cheekbones.

"I am sorry, mother, but really! I knew no good would come of that association. I hope Hayward does beat the scoundrel!"

"But some good did come of it, George," Lady Atherton pointed out gently. "Belle turned him down flat!"

His gaze gentled as it settled on his sister again. "Good for you, Belle. What would you like to do this evening? I am at your disposal."

An imp of mischief danced in her eyes as

she said, "I would like *you* to take me to the mas-querade at Vauxhall, *dear* George."

"You little minx!" He laughed. "But it won't do, Belle, really. The anonymity of these mas-querades usually ensures they turn into sad romps!"

"But you will be there to protect me, George, and as I will also be afforded anonymity, no one will be any the wiser."

George turned to his mother for support.

Lady Atherton cast her eyes up to heaven. "Oh, take her, George, or we will never hear the end of it! Just make sure you keep a very close eye on her."

Belle let out an undignified squeal, pushed back her chair, and rushed around the table to give her mother an affectionate hug.

"You are the best mother in the world," she said, and then hastily left the room before she could change her mind.

George gave his mother an exasperated glance. "This, I suppose, is another of those things that become more attractive when forbidden?"

Lady Atherton sighed and patted his hand. "Indeed. If she must attend such an event, I would rather she did so under your supervi-sion, George. Just make sure she does not remove her mask and do not let her out of your sight!"

Once she had gained the privacy of her chamber, Belle sat herself in the chair by her window and retrieved the letter from her reticule. She had only had time to skim its contents at the breakfast table.

Dearest Belle,

The dreaded event has occurred! Lord Banfield has declared himself, and although I have put him off, saying that I need a little time to consider his proposal, I am feeling quite desperate. I only know that I would rather throw myself in the river than become shackled to him for life, or be forced to watch my sisters married off whilst I dwindle into an old maid!

Finding myself in such dire straits, I know you will understand when I tell you that I turned to Mr Bradford for advice. Since the night of Lady Percival's ball, he has been a constant source of support and proved to be both sensitive and understanding of my situation. Mother has now refused to allow me to see him or anyone else until I give Lord Banfield the required answer. I am a prisoner in my own house!

I have been forced to subterfuge. Mr Bradford has managed to send me a brief note through my maid. He has asked me to plead a headache to Mama and then sneak out and accompany him to the masquerade at Vauxhall tonight. I feel quite dreadful at committing such a deception, but I must overcome such feelings as he has assured me that he has a plan for my immediate relief. I hardly dare believe this can be so, but even though our acquaintance has only recently blossomed into a deeper friendship, I feel sure I can rely on him.

I must admit, however, that I feel in need of some support. Although I hesitate to drag you into such an improper situation, my very dear friend, if you feel you could perhaps also sneak away, I would be very grateful for your support in my hour of need. I will be wearing a pink domino and mask. Please do try to come.

Yours in desperation,

Lydia.

Belle let out a long, troubled sigh. She was not concerned that Mr Bradford had transferred his affections. Indeed, she had hoped that he might, and that he might also prove to be the solution to Lydia's problems. However, she could not see how it could be achieved in such a scrambling way. If Lydia had just held firm and refused Lord Banfield's offer, although she would have almost certainly been subjected to some unpleasantness, she felt sure her mother would not have removed her from town. It was no mean expense to fund a come out, and she could not imagine that Mrs Pargeter would have given up the hope of establishing her daughter so easily. Once the disappointment of losing an earl had passed, Mr Bradford's suit might have become quite acceptable to her, but if Lydia's deception were discovered, there would be no hope of such a satisfactory conclusion!

Feeling the need to stop her friend from making what she felt sure would be a dreadful mistake, she crossed to her writing desk and picked up her quill. However, after nibbling the end pensively for a few seconds, she threw it down again. A moment's reflection was enough to convince her that if Lydia really was being watched so closely, the chances were any letters directed to her would be intercepted. No, she could not risk putting anything down on paper.

Jumping decisively to her feet, she rang for her maid. She would pay her a morning call. Even though Lydia claimed she was not allowed to see anyone, Belle knew she was prone to exaggeration. If she could just see her, perhaps she could persuade her not to take such a potentially damaging step.

However, when she sent in her calling card, the butler informed her that Miss Pargeter was not at home. It seemed that in this case, she had not exaggerated after all. She would have to hope that her subterfuge remained undiscovered.

Worry over her friend's predicament, whilst

dampening her excitement at attending the masquerade, could not completely extinguish it. And as soon as they passed through the land entrance into the gardens, she found herself cast into transports of delight. Never, in her wildest imaginings, had she imagined the scene that met her incredulous gaze. The break in the bad weather had ensured the gardens were well attended, and the air was alive with the hum of voices and the tinkle of laughter.

Hoards of people dressed in the most fantastical costumes thronged the gravelled walks that surrounded the main glade, and wandering performers weaved their way amongst them, juggling, performing acrobatics, or even swallowing fire. Around a central octagonal temple that housed a large orchestra, Greek gods and goddesses, devils, harlequins, nuns, monks, sultans, and Cossacks, whirled and twirled with gay abandon in a confusion of noise, colour, and movement. Belle felt she had stepped into a play or an exotic dream. Coloured lamps hung from the trees and colonnades that framed the glade, casting an otherworldly glow over the whole.

"Oh, George," she exclaimed. "Thank you. I would not have missed this for the world!"

Her brother drew her arm through his own, his grey eyes glittering behind his black mask.

"Stay close, Belle. The donning of a disguise often breeds a sense of freedom in the wearer which causes them to throw off the restraints of decency and decorum that usually operate so powerfully in a more restrained setting."

At that moment, a rather scantily clad shepherdess emerged from the Turkish tent that housed an array of refreshments. She picked up her skirts, revealing two slender ankles, and ran past them giggling, before disappearing down a dimly lit walk, closely followed by a portly Turkish sultan.

"I see what you mean," Belle said in a hushed voice, her eyes huge behind her scarlet mask.

"At least you are wearing the only scarlet domino that I can see, so I will not lose you easily."

They skirted the glade for a while, content to observe the amazing characters. They were forced to pause as a huge hooded monk came to a halt before them. His face was thrown into darkness by the deep hood of his cowl, making him look quite sinister. After regarding them in an unnerving silence for a moment or two, he offered them a small bow before standing aside to let them pass. Belle let out a nervous giggle.

"How strange it is, not to know who anyone is!"

"There is usually an unmasking at midnight, but we will be gone before then. I have arranged for the coach to pick us up at eleven-thirty. It is imperative that you remain incognito!"

A small frown marred Belle's brow as a sudden thought occurred to her.

"What is it?" her observant brother asked.

Belle was beginning to realise how difficult it would be to find Lydia in the melee of disguised people. She would need George's help. Bracing herself for his disapproval, she reluctantly re-vealed the real purpose of her visit.

They had come to a line of private supper boxes. The back of each was lined with paint-ings of various pastoral or mythological scenes. He led her into one, signalling for a passing waiter to bring them some refreshment.

"I might have known you had embroiled yourself in some scrape or other!" he said, pulling forward a chair for her.

"It is not *my* scrape, George. And I tried to call on Lydia to dissuade her from taking such a rash step, but I was told she was not at home!"

He had begun to drum his fingers on the supper table, a sure sign he was not best pleased.

"If you had only informed me of the purpose of this expedition earlier, I could have told you at the outset that it would be a fruitless exercise. You may as well look for a needle in a haystack."

Belle nodded a trifle disconsolately. "I am beginning to realise that now," she admitted. "But, George, I must make a push to find her and persuade her to return home before her absence is discovered!"

The waiter returned, bringing an array of dishes. Belle nibbled at a slice of wafer thin ham and took a cautious sip from the glass of rack punch she had been served.

"Go carefully with that, Belle," warned George. "It is deceptively strong, and you will need all your wits about you if we are to have any chance of finding your friend."

"Oh, so you will help! George, you are the best of brothers!"

"Well, your intentions were good, after all," he said gruffly. "Miss Pargeter is either a hoyden or a very silly young lady. She is lucky to have you as a friend. I don't suppose she informed you what she would be wearing?"

"Indeed, she did. A pink domino."

"That is something, at least. If Bradford wishes to be private with her, I suggest we check the supper boxes first and then try some of the walks if that fails."

Belle immediately rose to her feet. "Let us go at once, George. The sooner we find her, the better."

The boxes were half empty as it was still quite early for supper. A lady in a pink, silk domino, occupied none of them. As they passed the last box, Belle's gaze was drawn to the occupants. Two gentlemen faced each over the supper table, but rather than any tempting morsels of food, a large parcel wrapped in brown paper lay between them. They were an unlikely couple. One was dressed as a harlequin, but the other had made little effort with his disguise. He wore a worn coat that had been patched in more than one place, the lower part of his face was obscured by a muffler, and a rather battered hat was pulled low over his head.

A voice that she thought sounded vaguely familiar floated towards her.

"You have done well, Gibbs. Meet me near the land gate in an hour."

"Come along, Belle! Do you want to find your friend or not?" George said tetchily.

Belle quickened her steps to catch up with him. Leaving the main glade, they began to make their way down one of the gravelled walk-

ways. The paths were largely straight and con-
nected at right angles. At times giggles could be
heard coming from behind trees or bushes. At
these moments, George took Belle's arm and
hastily hurried her past. After twenty minutes or
so, they had still had no luck.

"This is ridiculous," George finally said. "We
could look all night and not find them!"

Belle was beginning to agree with him. They
had just turned into another walkway when they
came across a kiosk. It was a fairly small structure covered in brightly striped canvas. The
front flap was pulled back, and inside an old
gypsy woman sat smoking a pipe.

"Like me to tell your fortune, my pretty?"
she said in a low, rasping voice.

Belle's feet had begun to ache, and the idea
of sitting down for a few minutes seemed very
attractive. She paused and looked at her brother.
"May I?"

He sighed and looked down at her for a long
moment. "It is all nonsense, you know, we make
our own fortune."

A harsh cackle came from the gypsy. "For
good or ill, but only those as can read the signs
can make the most of their opportunities."

"Well, nonsense or not, I think it might be
interesting."

George threw a silver coin onto the small table inside the kiosk. The gypsy shot out a hand and pocketed it in a flash.

"Do not be long, Belle," George warned. "My patience is wearing very thin." He strode over to a nearby tree, folded his arms, and leaned nonchalantly against its trunk.

Belle ducked inside the low entrance and took the seat across the table from the old lady. The gypsy reached for the walking stick beside her and flipped the string that held the flap open. Belle suddenly felt a little uneasy. Only one small lamp lit the interior. It shone directly on her. The gypsy woman was thrown into shade, and Belle could not see her face clearly.

"Cards or ball?" she muttered.

"Cards," Belle replied softly.

A gnarled hand reached for a greasy looking deck. Belle noticed that her knuckles were swollen, and her nails long and not overly clean. She shuffled the pack with some difficulty and then laid the cards on the table. Belle's eyes became riveted on them as she slowly turned the first card. It was the eleven of spades.

"Ah, you are involved in a foolish intrigue, my dear," the gypsy said.

Belle's eyes flew to hers, but the gypsy was

focussed solely upon the cards. The next re-vealed the ten of hearts, reversed.

"It is causing you some slight anxiety."

Belle gasped. The following card, the knave of diamonds, was also reversed.

"All becomes clearer. Beware an unfaithful friend who will be the cause of some mischief."

Then came the knave of spades reversed. The gypsy paused for a moment, and Belle felt the unseen eyes upon her. "I see a dark man who is also plotting some mischief. Not the one who accompanied you, my dear, but you need to be careful."

Belle gulped. The knave was supplanted with the king of hearts.

"This is better," the gypsy murmured. "I see a fair, trustworthy man who may be of help to you."

For some reason, Lord Hayward's visage swam into her mind.

"Go on," she breathed.

The final card was the ace of clubs. "Either joy, money, or good news is coming your way, my pretty."

Belle felt a little relieved; this was more the sort of glib re-assurance she had expected.

Rising to her feet, she smiled at the hunched

figure before her. "Well, on that point, I hope you may be proved to be correct."

"Oh, I will, my pretty, I will. On all counts. It is both a gift and a curse."

Pushing the canvas out of the way, Belle stepped back onto the path.

"There, George, that did not take too long." As she straightened she realised she was talking to herself. The path was, for the moment, empty, and of George there was no sign. She walked forwards a few steps, beginning to feel a little nervous. "Come out, George," she said. "You are not amusing!"

Suddenly she felt an arm snake around her waist. "George, you beast!" she exclaimed, turning swiftly.

It was not, however, George, but a stranger in a shepherd's costume. Judging by the way he was swaying, he had imbibed far too freely of the punch.

"I will be your George if you so desire, fair maiden," he slurred, pulling her closer against him.

A disgusting mix of alcohol fumes and bad breath sent Belle reeling backwards, but not before she had given him an unladylike shove. It was all that was needed to send the shepherd toppling. He fell in an ungainly heap on the path. Lifting her skirts, she turned and fled down another walk, but not before the cackling laugh of the gypsy came to her ears.

Only when her breath was coming in painful short gasps, did she slow to a walk. Here the trees met overhead and the lanterns were much diminished, only the occasional light casting its furtive, flickering rays a few yards ahead, throwing the rest of the path into even deeper shadow. Belle felt she had stepped out of a dream and into a nightmare. Somewhere nearby an owl hooted causing her to let out a small shriek. She was, she realised, hopelessly lost and being ridiculously missish. A sudden vision of herself as Little Red Riding Hood made her grit her teeth and give a small, hard laugh.

"Beware all wolves, for I am no child to be devoured," she whispered.

Pausing to gather herself and knit the ends of her shredded nerves, she tried to gain her bearings. George had said that he had ordered the coach to meet them at the land gate at eleven-thirty, if she could only find her way there, he was sure to find her. A shadow, darker than all the rest began to take shape in front of her. As she came closer, she realised it was a small temple. Perhaps there would be someone there who could direct her. She soon reached it and ran up the shallow steps that led to the entrance. Exercising a little caution, she slowed as she reached the entrance and listened carefully. When no sound greeted her, she tiptoed inside. A single lamp lit the interior, but otherwise, the temple was empty. Feeling slightly deflated, she turned to go but paused as a flash of colour caught her eye. Stepping over to the bench seat that ran around the wall of the structure, she reached for the object that had caught her interest. It was a pink, silk loo mask.

"Lydia," she whispered.

Her fears fled as she was filled with new resolution. Lydia had been here, she was sure of it! But what could have occurred to cause her to flee the temple in such a hurry that she had left her mask behind? If she were recognised her game would certainly be up! It would be disastrous and her hopes of forming any desirable connection, hopeless.

Belle ran lightly back down the steps and made her way in what she hoped was the general direction of the land entrance. Her instincts served her well. The lights became more frequent, and in a break in the trees, she saw the pavilion that was near the gate in the distance and caught sight of a pink domino. Thankfully, Lydia had her hood pulled up. She appeared to be on the arm of Mr Bradford, judging by the flash of blond hair that was tied back in a black ribbon.

Her path ran parallel to the one leading to the gate. Picking up her skirts, she left it and ran through the trees to reach the one that would take her more directly to her destination. Her eyes were so fixed on the receding figure in the pink domino, that she did not see the protruding tree root that sent her sprawling in the grass. She landed with a thump, and all the breath was knocked from her. Even so, she tried to rise, but a sharp pain darted from her ankle and shot up her leg. She gave a muffled moan and suddenly found her mouth covered by a large hand. She had had enough! She bit down hard on the fingers covering her mouth and did not stop until she felt the faintly metallic taste of blood fill her mouth. The hand remained clamped to her lips, but a faint familiar voice whispered in her ear.

"Although I admire your prompt action, Lady Isabella, I would be grateful if you would desist."

She turned her head sharply to find herself staring up into the shadowed visage of the monk. Lord Hayward! The hand was removed from her mouth, and he placed one finger over his lips in a warning gesture. He nodded to a

65

clump of trees just ahead of them. Belle squinted through the dim light and could just make out part of a harlequin costume.

"That was not part of our agreement," growled a low voice. "Money on delivery, that was our terms."

"I was hardly going to bring so large a sum to a gathering such as this," another voice drawled.

Belle's eyes widened as she now placed the voice she had heard earlier. Lord Sandford!

"I have become aware that I was being followed at least three times in the last week, hence the need for our meeting here. I challenge anyone to find me amongst the motley array of characters that are here tonight. I will, however, take the painting. You may come to the tradesman's entrance of my townhouse tomorrow evening. Shall we say eight o'clock? I will, by then, have concluded some other trifling business I must attend to and will have the payment ready."

"Just make sure that you do," came the disgruntled reply. "Or there will be trouble!"

"I do not like threats." The voice remained soft but held a hint of menace.

The clown then strode off in the direction of the gate with the package tucked beneath his

gaudy cloak. A few moments later, his companion disappeared in the other direction.

Belle was full of questions, but she had not
forgotten her friend.

"Lord Hayward, I must get to the gate.
Please, help me, for my ankle is turned. I must
reach my friend before she leaves!" she said, in a
low voice full of urgency.

Wasting no time on words, Lord Hayward
helped her to her feet and slipped an arm
around her waist. He lifted her into his arms and
with no more ado, strode purposefully towards
the gate. When they passed through, they found
a line of waiting carriages, but Belle could see
no sign of Lydia or George.

"You can put me down now," Belle said, a
little shyly.

Lord Hayward lowered her gently to her
feet. "Can you see your friend?"

Belle shook her head and turned to a short
man with an overly large head, who seemed to
be greeting people as they came and went.

"Oh, sir, have you seen a lady in a pink
domino pass through?" she asked.

He removed his silver beaver hat, bowed low,
and beamed at her. "Mr Simpson, at your service, ma'am. I have indeed seen such a lady as
you describe, she departed not so many minutes

since, in a hired post-chaise. I believe I heard the young gentleman give the instruction to head for The Great North Road."

"Where could they be going?" Belle mused aloud.

Lord Hayward swept her back into his arms and looked down at her intently for a moment. There was no sign of sleepiness in his eyes now, on the contrary, they were sharp and clear. "I fear there is an elopement afoot. Do you wish to stop them?"

"Yes, I cannot think what she is about. There will be such a scandal!" Her voice sounded breathless even to her own ears, and she found her heart was thudding in her ears.

He began to stride off towards a waiting curricle. Belle twisted awkwardly in his arms and turned back towards Mr Simpson. "If a man in a black domino asks for me, tell him not to worry, I am with—"

"A friend," interrupted Lord Hayward. "We have your reputation to consider also, my lady."

"Oh, but no one can know who I am."

"Let us hope that is so," he said, lifting her into his curricle.

"Thank you, James, but I don't think I will be needing you," he said apologetically to his tiger, cracking his whip with some authority.

His perfectly matched bays swept forwards majestically. As they raced swiftly through the streets, Belle gathered her scattered thoughts.

"You must wonder what I was doing at Vauxhall," she said in a small voice.

"Satisfying your curiosity, I should imagine," he said dryly. And then added in a gentler tone, "And trying to aid a friend, I imagine Miss Pargeter. I must admit I am surprised your brother would set out on such an expedition."

Belle looked up at him in surprise. "It appears I do not need to explain anything, after all, sir. You seem to have worked it all out in a trice. I am afraid I am not so astute, however."

"Would you mind very much, Lady Isabella, if I explained it all to you tomorrow, after my race? If we are to catch the love-struck couple, I must concentrate on the chase. They have four horses and a start on us, you know."

"Of course," Belle said.

Her eyes widened, and she clapped a hand to her mouth.

"Oh, Lord Hayward, your hand! Have I hurt it dreadfully? Will it affect your race tomorrow?"

"It is nothing," he said smoothly. "And as you see, I can drive unhindered."

It was true, he was driving at speed, yet he

handled his team with such ease that she did not feel at all unsafe.

"I have one more request, my dear."

"Name it," she replied promptly.

"I imagine you will have some explanations to give later, and whilst I do not wish you to lie to your mother or brother, might I suggest you, shall we say, forget about the harlequin for tonight?"

Belle was hopelessly intrigued but felt she owed Lord Hayward her loyalty.

"Consider it forgotten." A mischievous smile curved her lips. "But only for tonight. I expect you to visit me after your race tomorrow and explain it all."

"Oh, I intend to," he assured her.

They both lapsed into silence. It occurred to Belle that she really ought to feel at least a little apprehensive to be racing through the night with a gentleman that she really did not know that well, yet she did not. Lord Hayward seemed to take everything in his stride with a calmness that she was beginning to realise had little to do with placidity.

They soon left the environs of the metropolis behind and began to make their way across Finchley Common. It was fortunate that the moon had made an appearance to light their way, casting its eerie glow across the wide expanse of open land. As they approached the small hamlet at Brown's Wells, Lord Hayward slowed his horses and turned into the yard of The Green Man Inn.

"I will make some enquiries here. I would like to know how far ahead..." he suddenly broke off, for in the yard stood a bright yellow chaise.

"I think we have found them," he murmured. Jumping down, he tossed a coin to a stable lad. "If I am not back in ten minutes, walk them for me, will you?"

Without waiting for an answer, he lifted Belle down and set her gently on her feet, offering her his arm for support. "Is it very painful?" he asked, solicitously.

"It is throbbing a little," she admitted, "but I can manage."

On enquiring for the travellers who had arrived in the post-chaise, the innkeeper gave them an amazed look. It was not every day that a monk travelling with a lady in a red domino and loo mask visited his establishment. "I knew there was something smoky going on and no mistake," he muttered. "They are taking refreshment in the private parlour." He nodded to a door opposite the taproom.

The scene that met their eyes was worthy of the best melodrama. Lydia sat on a low chair by the fire, sobbing uncontrollably, one hand covering her eyes, her head turned away from Mr Bradford, who knelt before her, clutching her remaining free hand in both of his own. He jumped to his feet when they entered the room, his eyes widening in alarm.

"Lord Hayward! And, is it you, Lady Isabella?"

So much for her disguise! Lydia's sobbing stopped mid-flow, and her head snapped around at the words.

"Belle!" she cried, bursting into tears once more. She hurried across the room and launched herself into her friend's arms with such force, only Lord Hayward's quick presence of mind prevented both of them overbalancing. He stepped swiftly behind Belle, putting his hands at her waist to steady her. Finding herself pressed to a chest as unyielding as rock, Belle managed to push her friend away.

"Calm yourself, Lydia," she said sternly.

"How can I?" Lydia cried. "Everything has g-gone s-so h-horribly wrong."

"It was not my fault, my love!" Mr Bradford said pleadingly, wringing his hands in anguish.

Lydia rounded on her hapless rescuer. "Not

72

your fault?" she screeched. "You shower me with promises to cherish and protect me, persuade me to sneak from my home like a thief in the night, then elope with you in no more than I stand up in, before informing me that you have been so careless as to have had your pocket picked and cannot so much as pay our shot here, never mind take us one mile further!"

Mr Bradford blanched before his 'loves' harsh words. "But, my dearest Lydia," he protested, taking her hands in his. Before he could say more, a loud querulous voice penetrated the room.

"Of course you have a private parlour free, man. I want some supper now! I am devilishly sharp-set I tell you!"

The door of the parlour opened on these words, and Lord Banfield strode into the room.

Lydia screamed and then fainted clean away in Mr Bradford's conveniently waiting arms.

Ever the loyal friend, Belle cast wildly about in her mind for a way to explain the extraordinary situation to the newest arrival, but before she could utter a word, the landlord followed him in.

"That's them, my lord, rolled up in a yellow-bounder not half an hour ago. I knew there was something smoky about them! The postboy informs me they be heading for Gretna and no mistake! As for these two, for a man who has pledged himself to the service of God to be involved in such shenanigans, is shameful, just shameful!"

It seemed that Lord Banfield had suddenly lost his appetite, for after staring at his unconscious intended for a moment or two, he turned on his heel and left the room without a word.

"Look after your friend," murmured Lord Hayward, following the landlord from the room. He closed the door firmly behind him as more than one head was peering around the door of the taproom in an effort to discover what all the to-do was about.

"Oh, lay her down on the sofa, Mr Bradford," Belle said shortly. Then with no more ado, she knelt beside her friend and gave her a none too gentle shake.

Lydia moaned, and her eyes fluttered open. "Has he gone?" she whispered.

"Yes," said Belle, turning to Mr Bradford. "Might I suggest you order some wine?"

But even as she spoke, there was a knock at the door. A serving girl bustled in with the required refreshments. "Compliments of the monk," she giggled.

"That will be all, thank you," Belle said

sternly, as she saw the girl's eyes drinking in every detail of the scene before her.

"Oh, take your mask off, Belle, do," Lydia said, sitting up and accepting the glass of wine from Mr Bradford.

"No, I don't think I will," replied Belle, rising gingerly to her feet before sitting next to her friend. "If you had kept yours on, you might have kept your identity hidden from Lord Banfield. What possessed you to leave it behind?"

Lydia's eyes flew to Mr Bradford, and a surge of colour warmed her cheeks.

"I see," said Belle dryly. "Well, you have made a sad mull of everything and no mistake."

Seemingly exhausted by her recent histrionics, Lydia simply pouted and took a sip of her wine.

"We must hope Lord Hayward can help us salvage something from this situation," Belle said a trifle doubtfully.

Lydia looked more hopeful. "Oh, Belle, do you think he can?"

That esteemed gentleman returned to the room at that moment and offered Belle a reassuring smile, but it was Mr Bradford who he addressed.

"I have paid off your postboy. He is waiting

to take you back to Town. I suggest you leave now."

Belle thought she saw a flicker of relief cross Mr Bradford's pale features. However, it seemed he was not ready to dismiss the image of himself as a romantic figure rescuing a persecuted damsel, quite yet, for he straightened his slumped shoulders and stood his ground. "I thank you for your kind offer, sir, but I cannot leave Miss Pargeter in such a precarious position."

Lord Hayward took a step closer to the young man. He towered over him, and when he spoke, he did so in a hard, biting tone that Belle had never heard him use before.

"If Miss Pargeter is in a precarious position, it is because you have placed her there. I have managed to persuade Lord Banfield that it would not be in his interests to spread this sordid tale abroad, as for his intended to flee with a green upstart of no great fortune or standing, rather than accept his proposal, would make him a laughing stock. He will accept Miss Pargeter's refusal of his offer with good grace, and retire to the country a trifle earlier than expected. He would be well within his rights to call you out, you young fool, and although he may be rather stout, there is nothing wrong with his firing arm. I have seen him culp a wafer more than once at Mantons."

"Oh, but Lord Hayward, I can't…" Lydia began.

Lord Hayward's incredulous gaze cut her short. "Oh, I think you will find after a little reflection, Miss Pargeter, that you most certainly can. Your behaviour has been selfish, thoughtless, and rash. Not content to whip your friend's admirer from under her nose, you then embroil yourself in a shameless deception and encourage your friend to do the same. Added to this, you have scorned an honourable proposal from a gentleman whose only crime against you has been his fervent desire to make you his wife, and all because you have not the backbone to simply decline his offer. After inflicting such a humiliation on Lord Banfield, he has no wish to see you again, but will expect to receive your letter declining his gracious offer in the morning."

Never, had a gentleman addressed Lydia in such a manner. She once more burst into noisy, hysterical tears. Unimpressed, Lord Hayward turned back to Mr Bradford.

"Are you still here?" he said softly. "If you are not gone before I count to five, you will be forcibly removed."

He reached no more than two before Mr

Bradford departed with all due haste. Lord Hayward reached for a glass of wine and drained it in one great gulp.

"Where is this monk?" an angry voice roared from the corridor.

Lord Hayward settled himself against the corner of the table and folded his arms with weary patience.

Moments later, George strode into the parlour, his fists clenched and his face like thunder.

He took in the scene before him in one comprehensive glance, his expression twisting into a grimace as Miss Pargeter's noisy sobs reached his ears. "Hayward!" he said incredulously. "Do not tell me you are the monk who abducted my sister!"

Lord Hayward held out a glass of burgundy to him. "Yes, I know that you would like nothing better than to bloody my nose, Althorpe, but apart from the fact that I doubt you could do it, I really do not deserve it, you know."

Belle's brows shot up at the transformation in him. Once again he was the sleepy-eyed gentleman with the placid demeanour. Putting that aside to ponder on later, she rose awkwardly and limped a few steps forwards.

"Belle," George said quickly, ignoring the

wine and coming hastily towards her. "You are hurt!"

"It is nothing," she said, taking his hands. "We are in Lord Hayward's debt. I twisted my ankle and he found me. We followed Lydia here. But what happened to you? When I came out of the gypsy's booth, you were gone!"

"A case of mistaken identity," he said shortly. "Would you believe there was another lady in a scarlet domino, after all? I had not been paying attention, and then I suddenly spotted her in the distance. I assumed it was you. By the time I had realised my mistake and returned, you were nowhere to be seen! And that old crone was no help! My only hope was that you would wait for me at the land gate, but a queer looking gentleman informed me you had been carried out by a monk and disappeared off in his curricle, heading for the Great North Road!"

"Oh dear, what a comedy of errors!" Belle smiled, the twinkle back in her eye. "But do sit down, George, and I will explain everything."

CHAPTER 4

W hen they finally returned home, after delivering an ungrateful Lydia into the arms of her incredulous and quite hysterical mother, who boxed her ears soundly before dragging her inside the house, they had to relate the whole tale to Lady Atherton, who had waited up for them.

She listened with all her characteristic calmness, even managing a small smile when Belle mimicked the outraged tones of the amazed innkeeper. She nevertheless turned a stern gaze upon both her children when they had finally finished.

"Although the quality of loyalty is generally to be admired, Belle, do you not think it might have been better to have informed me of this proposed elopement?" she said in her gentle way. "I might then have warned Mrs Pargeter of the impending event and nipped it in the bud." She let that sink in for a moment before adding fairly, "Although, perhaps things have turned out for the best, after all. Lydia's mother is an ambitious, vulgar woman who prizes wealth above all things. At least, now, she cannot force Lydia into a match, I must admit, I would not want for you, Belle."

She then turned her attention to her son. "And as for you, George, I do believe I warned you not to let Belle out of your sight, even for a moment?"

He made no move to defend himself but accepted his culpability with a nod.

"However," she continued, "things could have been worse. I am a little surprised that Lord Hayward was attending such an event, but I can only be grateful that he was. It seems to me that he behaved in a very gentlemanly manner, towards you, at least, Belle."

"Indeed, he was all that is good," she acknowledged. "I only hope the late night will not affect the outcome of his race tomorrow. He has promised to pay me a visit to let me know the outcome."

"I am glad to hear it, Belle, for then I can

thank him personally."

It was perhaps not surprising that after all the exciting events of the evening, Belle fell almost immediately into a deep, dreamless sleep.

Her ankle was still quite swollen and throbbed quite dreadfully in the morning, and so Lady Atherton sent for the doctor.

He and Belle were old friends. He had it bandaged in a trice but gave her a knowing look over the rim of his spectacles. "Nothing too serious, little Miss Quicksilver," he assured her. "But you will have to keep it up for a few days, you know. No outings *at all* until the swelling goes down! And it would be better if you remained in bed today."

"But Doctor Newton, there is nothing I hate more than staying in bed!"

He smiled sympathetically down at her, his brown eyes twinkling merrily. "I wonder how many times I have heard that refrain over the years?"

Belle grinned back. "But I have been very good of late," she pointed out. "It must be all of two years since I have seen you!"

"Why, yes, I do believe you are right." He smiled. "Let me see, I think the last time you had fallen out of a tree trying to rescue a cat. What happened this time?"

Belle shook her head saucily. "I cannot tell you I am afraid, Doctor Newton, it is a secret!"

He chuckled. "Ah, I see. A mystery, eh? Makes it more interesting than admitting you fell down a rabbit hole, I suppose."

"Just so," confirmed Lady Atherton who had been hovering in the background. "But you can be quite sure we will take every care of her, Doctor Newton, I assure you."

"Of course," he bowed. "You always do, ma'am, you always do."

Lady Atherton knew Belle would fret herself to flinders if she were forced to stay in her bed. She had a footman carry her down to the drawing room as soon as the good doctor had gone, insisting, however, that she remained stretched out on one of the sofas in the drawing room.

Belle tried to occupy herself by reading Sense and Sensibility, written by an anonymous Lady, but found she could not maintain her concentration for long enough to follow the story. The words of the gypsy kept floating into her mind. *I see a dark man who is also plotting some mischief.* Whilst it seemed clear she must have been referring to Lord Sandford, she could not imagine what he had been up to. Why was he being followed? What was the significance of the painting he had so furtively acquired? And most intriguing of all, what had Lord Hayward got to do with it all?

After a light nuncheon, her mother joined her, again taking up the sewing she had abandoned a few nights before.

"What are you making, Mama?" she asked languidly.

"Just a nightshirt for little George." She smiled. "He is growing so fast! I cannot quite credit that he is already two. I am hoping Harriet will bring the boys for an extended stay when we return to Atherton."

Belle smiled as she thought of her practical, no-nonsense elder sister. "Harriet seems very happy with Sir Thomas, don't you think?"

"Oh, yes," agreed Lady Atherton. "Your father took a little persuading as to his suitability at first, but once he saw how settled and happy she was, he soon persuaded himself that it was all his idea in the first place!"

Belle laughed. "How very like Papa."

"He will be just as happy for you when you are settled, Belle," she said gently.

Belle blushed but was saved the necessity of answering as Radcliffe entered the room.

"Would you be at home to a Mrs Pargeter, ma'am?" He was as impassive as ever, but the very slight emphasis he gave to the name, hinted that he perhaps doubted it.

"Oh Lord!" muttered Belle, swinging her feet to the ground.

"Stay where you are, dear," Lady Atherton said firmly. "Give us a brief moment, Radcliffe, and then show her in."

She put her sewing away quickly, hiding her workbasket behind her chair and then brought a footstool to Belle. "Rest your foot on here, Belle, you will feel a little more dignified."

Noting Belle's slightly alarmed expression, she offered her a small smile. "Do not worry, my child, you may leave Mrs Pargeter to me."

Mrs Pargeter entered the room a few moments later. She was a plain, plump woman with close-set eyes and a rather pinched mouth. Her complexion was pale and was made rather sallow by the amazing concoction she wore over her primped, mousy locks. It was a bonnet fashioned of yellow satin, trimmed with a wide band, also of yellow satin, that was tied in a large bow at the front. In addition to this, two huge yellow ostrich feathers were placed behind the bow.

Belle blinked, and for a moment, could look at nothing else. It was quite extraordinary and in her opinion, quite hideous. Perhaps she thought it made her appear taller, for she was indeed, very short. Her diminutive stature, did not, however, house a timid or meek spirit.

Mrs Pargeter stood for a moment, her steely gaze sweeping around the room as if assessing the worth of every item.

Lady Atherton bowed her head graciously. "Mrs Pargeter, please take a seat. You must forgive Lady Isabella not rising to greet you, but as you see, she is somewhat indisposed."

Mrs Pargeter's hard beady eyes swivelled towards Belle. "Indeed? She is fortunate to have only hurt her ankle and not her reputation."

Lady Atherton raised one haughty eyebrow, annoyed at her lack of finesse. It seemed the gloves were off already.

"Ah, I think you must be referring to the children's expedition to Vauxhall last evening. It is indeed a pity that they chose the night of a masquerade to visit, but no great harm need come of it, I am sure."

Mrs Pargeter's pale cheeks were swiftly suffused with a bright pink tint that clashed horribly with her bonnet. Refusing to take the dignified way out offered to her, however, her small, pinched mouth opened on a gasp. "No great harm? No great harm?" she spluttered. "How can you say such a thing, ma'am, when my daughter has lost the certain chance of a very desirable connection?"

It seemed Mrs Pargeter was determined to have it all out regardless of the unforgiving light that would be shone upon her own family.

"That is indeed unfortunate for you, Mrs Pargeter. Although it does not seem that the connection was quite so desirable to your daughter," Lady Atherton said gently. "Indeed, it cannot have been for her to have attempted to elope in such a foolish fashion when I am sure all she had needed to have done, was to explain her misgivings to her understanding mama."

"Understanding mama?" her visitor spluttered. "It is easy for you, ma'am, to make light of the situation when your daughter has almost every fool claiming to be a gentleman, fawning at her feet! It would not surprise me if she..." she paused to point an accusatory finger in Belle's direction. "*She*," she repeated in bitter tones, "encouraged Lydia in her outrageous behaviour!"

Mrs Pargeter had now gone too far. Lady Atherton's eyes flashed, but Mrs Pargeter had worked herself into such an agitated state she did not heed the warning but carried on heedlessly.

"Probably jealous that my Lydia had received a proposal before she, the daughter of an earl, had enjoyed that felicity, and that's the truth!"

Lady Atherton rose to her feet and looked scathingly at her visitor. "If it is the truth you wish for, Mrs Pargeter, it is the truth you shall have," she said, in steely tones that brooked no interruption. "I have listened to your vulgar display of unrestrained emotion and baseless accusations long enough. The ugly, unvarnished truth, is that your social climbing ambitions have overridden your motherly instincts if indeed you have any, which I take leave to doubt! They have led you to encourage a suitor, who is almost old enough to be your daughter's father and has nothing to greatly recommend him apart from his wealth and title, regardless of her wishes. These actions forced her into a precipitate flight with the first gentleman who showed her a sympathetic ear, an action, I admit, I would hope any girl raised with firm principles or any female delicacy would avoid like the plague! My daughter has only ever acted in Lydia's best interests. When her sound advice to simply refuse the prospective offer was ignored, and she discovered that Lydia intended to attend the masquerade with Mr Bradford, (and that is *all* she knew), she decided she must go herself, putting her own reputation, as you say, at risk. But all in an attempt to persuade Lydia to go home at once! She, at least, went with the escort of her brother. Unfortunately, she lost him for a few moments and it was then she saw your daughter. Once she discovered what she was up to, she risked her reputation further by flying through the night with Lord Hayward, who happened to be close by, in an effort to put a stop to such a rash, scandalous act. Fortunately for you, they succeeded. If Lydia has led you to believe anything else, she is a conscienceless little baggage!"

Mrs Pargeter was at last silenced. She regarded Lady Atherton in an amazed fashion, her small mouth agape.

Lady Atherton picked up a little bell from a nearby side-table and rang it quite forcefully. "Now, you may take your leave. I would just remind you, that it would be foolish indeed if any whisper of these unfortunate events were to circulate. Barely the only accurate statement you have made is that Lady Isabella is the daughter of an earl, and so I think you would find her version of events would carry considerably more weight than yours or Lydia's!"

As Radcliffe entered the room at that moment, with the excellent good timing to be expected of all good butlers, she was left with nothing to say. She was ushered masterfully out of the room without being quite sure how it came about. Only when the door was firmly closed behind her, did Lady Atherton sink gratefully into her chair.

"Mama," Belle breathed, her eyes huge in her face. "You were magnificent!"

Lady Atherton gave a shaky laugh. "I had hoped to have turned it all off with a light touch," she admitted ruefully. "But subtlety is clearly an unknown art to that preposterous quiz of a woman!"

As the day wore on, Belle became increasingly pensive and fidgety.

"What is on your mind, Belle?" asked Lady Atherton, a small smile playing about her lips.

"Oh, nothing really. But I cannot help wondering how Lord Hayward has fared in his race. I do hope he has won. It would be quite unfair if he were to be made a figure of fun when he is so good. He is worth ten of Lord Sandford!"

"I agree with you, my dear. But picking up and putting down that book a thousand times will not help you discover the outcome any faster."

The sound of a carriage outside in the street made Belle sit up a little straighter. She put a hand to her hair. "Is it him?" she asked quickly.

Sighing, her mother laid aside her sewing and moving over to the window that looked over the street, peeped through a small gap in the curtains.

"Yes, it is," she confirmed. "I must just go and make myself tidy. I won't be above a couple of moments, Belle."

She bustled out of the room, leaving Belle to receive their visitor.

Lord Hayward strode in a few moments later, without hurry, and offered Belle a deep bow. "I am glad to see you are taking care of that ankle, Lady Isabella."

"Never mind my stupid ankle, Lord Hayward. Please sit down and tell me at once, who won the race?"

As he settled himself comfortably into the chair her mother had so recently vacated, she noticed the bandage that encased one of his fingers. "Oh, I am so sorry, I do hope your injury did not affect the outcome!"

He offered her his sleepy smile, and she felt her heart turn over in her chest.

"Not at all. It was a close run thing, though. Lord Sandford is an excellent whip, but I think he must have been a little out of practice. I overtook him on the final stretch and just reached the finish line before him."

Belle clapped her hands in delight, and in her excitement forgot about her ankle. She tried to jump to her feet and stumbled as a swift, sharp stab of pain reminded her. Lord Hayward was out of his chair in a flash, catching her before she could fall.

Belle looked up into his face, her eyes widening and her stomach suddenly fluttering as if a thousand butterflies had been let loose there, as she saw the suddenly intent look in his blue eyes. Eyes that were not at all sleepy.

"Lady Isabella, would you do me the honour of becoming my wife?" he murmured gently, holding her close.

"Yes," she whispered. "Yes, please."

Her vision blurred as his face came closer to her own and he covered her lips in a soft, reverent kiss, before pulling her down onto the sofa and gently placing her foot back on the stool.

"You have made me the happiest of men," he said, kissing her hand.

She smiled shyly. "Even though I dragged you into a scrape?"

"It was my pleasure to extract you from it," he confirmed.

"Talking of scrapes, please, do tell me what you were doing at Vauxhall last night."

She listened in some amazement as Lord

Hayward disclosed his tale. Lord Sandford, it seemed, was involved in a painting smuggling ring. Apparently, he had received a couple of paintings from a group who had targeted the treasures being returned home from the Louvre and then had sold them on at a profit to private art collectors.

"But what have you got to do with it all?" she asked, bemused.

"I will tell you, Belle, but you must promise to keep it to yourself. It does not suit me that the world knows about my activities," he said seriously.

"Of course, Lord Hayward," she whispered, all agog.

"Please, call me Nathanial, or Nat if you prefer. I work for the government upon occasion and more recently, the war office, in particular."

"You are a spy?" she breathed.

He smiled. "Not exactly. Let us just say that when you are perceived as a sleepy, staid individual, that no one pays much attention to, people sometimes underestimate you, and you sometimes overhear things that others might not."

"As Lord Sandford underestimated you," she said. "What will become of him?"

"He is not of so much interest as those supplying him. Lord Liverpool wishes to foster good relations with our recent allies, who knows when we will need them again? By returning some of these paintings, that aim will be achieved. Fortunately, thanks to the conversation we overheard last night, we now have all the information we require and Lord Sandford is about to undergo an uncomfortable interview with Lord Liverpool himself. I think you will find he will disappear from society for quite some time."

"I am so glad I did not spoil everything for you," Belle said quietly.

Lord Hayward slipped his arm behind her shoulders. "Not only did you not spoil *anything* for me," he murmured, "you have made me the happiest man alive."

With that, he pulled her quite roughly into his arms and gave her a very thorough and satisfying kiss.

"Oh," she sighed, "I never knew a kiss could feel like that!"

He smiled and released her. "I should hope not."

"I hope this means what it should?" came a cool, collected voice from behind them.

Lord Hayward sprang to his feet at once. He gave Belle a sly wink before turning to face Lady Atherton. He bowed punctiliously, once more on his best behaviour. "Of course," he confirmed.

"I am happy to say that Lady Isabella has just consented to be my wife."

Lady Atherton quirked a brow. "Really? It appears that you have got things a trifle out of order, Lord Hayward. I had not thought you would be so impetuous."

Belle hid a smile as he managed to look very sheepish. "You are, of course, correct, ma'am. I don't know what came over me," he said, as if bemused. "But I can assure you I will make all haste to Atherton tomorrow, and seek your esteemed husband's approval in this matter."

Lady Atherton suddenly smiled. "Ah, well, much can be forgiven a man deeply in love. You have, at least, my approval, for what it is worth."

He bowed again. "I am honoured by your good opinion, Lady Atherton."

"In fact," she continued, "I think we will also return to Atherton. I am sure my husband will wish to consult Belle's wishes in this matter."

"Oh, but I do wish it, Mama," Belle assured her.

Lord Hayward stood aside as Lady Atherton went to embrace her daughter. "Then I am very happy for you, my dear."

The sound of a door banging was heard, and the next moment George strolled into the room. Not immediately perceiving Lord Hayward, he strolled over to his sister, and grinning, dropped a roll of readies into her lap.

"In a fit of madness and annoyance at Lord Sandford's audacious attempt to drag you to that infernal masquerade, I placed a bet on Hayward, after all. And would you believe it, he won? Sandford must be losing his touch. Apparently, Hayward took an outrageous risk on the final bend and overtook where no sane man would, catching the marquess off guard. He must have had a rush of blood to the head or something, for who would think such a slow-top would attempt such a thing?"

"George!" his mother said warningly. "That is no way to talk of your future brother-in-law. You had best make your apologies to Lord Hayward."

George quickly glanced up and coloured slightly. Striding forwards he shook his hand. "Congratulations, old chap. No offence intended."

"None taken," Lord Hayward assured him, casting an amused glance in the direction of his beloved, who was trying not to giggle. "I cannot imagine what came over me either. I really can't."

ABOUT THE AUTHOR

I love history and the Regency period in particular. I grew up on a diet of Jane Austen, Charlotte and Emily Bronte, and Georgette Heyer. Later, I put my love of reading to good use and gained a 1st class honours degree in literature.

I have been a teacher and tennis coach. I now write traditional Regency romance novels. I like to think my characters, though flawed, are likeable, strong, and true to the period. Writing has always been my dream and I am fortunate enough to have been able to realise that dream.

I live by the sea in Plymouth, England, with my partner, Dave. I like reading, sailing, wine, getting up early to watch the sunrise in summer, and long quiet evenings by the wood burner in our cabin on the cliffs in Cornwall in winter.

SAMPLE CHAPTER ROSALIND

LONDON 1818

The Earl of Atherton had played quite recklessly tonight, not really caring whether he won or lost. Each throw of the dice had been accomplished with a negligent flick of his deceptively strong wrist. The vast quantities of wine he had been drinking just as recklessly, only showed in his slightly sprawled posture and the stormy look in his half-veiled grey eyes. His winnings had mounted steadily before him yet he seemed as disinterested in this as in everything and everyone else around him.

"I think," he drawled softly, "yes, I really think that I have had enough."

This drew various amazed glances from the other gentlemen who shared the table.

"I say G-George," stammered the long-suffering gentleman to his left, "that's the outside of enough, r-really it is, when you've been fleecing us all m-mercilessly all night."

The wintry gaze gentled as the earl's glance rested on his old friend Lord Preeve, whose slightly unfocussed, protuberant wide-blue eyes resembled nothing more than that of a startled rabbit. His glorious golden locks (quite his best feature) which had earlier been lovingly arranged by his fastidious valet, were now wildly disordered due to the frustrated tugs he had been giving them as the dice fell against him time after time.

A weary but fond smile curved the earl's lips as he rose gracefully and began slowly pocketing the pile of carelessly flung notes and golden coins before him.

"My heart would be quite, quite wrung if I didn't know you were rich as Croesus," he murmured. "Go home, John, Wrencham will be looking for a new position if he catches sight of the disaster you have made of your hair. Even if he had sent you out coup au vent, which I am fairly certain, dear chap, he did not, he would be shocked, quite shocked."

This gentle ribbing drew a grin from his companion on the right. There was no malice in it and they all knew there was no danger of this prophesied event occurring; it would be a brave valet indeed who would leave the employ of so rich and generally easy going an employer.

"W-well really, G-George, I suppose Townsend has barely anything to s-say to that mad riot of chestnut curls you sport, eh?" he protested.

"Nothing at all, my dear John, they are quite natural I assure you," he reassured his spluttering friend. "Quite the bane of my sisters' lives if they are to be believed." He turned to the quiet, neatly dressed man next to him, quirking one finely drawn dark brow. "Coming, Philip?"

Sir Philip Bray, ex-captain of the 15th Hussars, had resigned his commission and reluctantly stepped into his late father's shoes on the occasion of his sad demise over a year ago. With rugged good looks, considerable charm and a natural aptitude for dancing, he was a firm favourite at every society function, yet despite countless lures having been thrown his way, had so far avoided the parson's mousetrap.

"With pleasure, my dear fellow, lead on," he smiled, pushing back his chair and getting only slightly unsteadily to his feet.

The steady drumming of some very white fingertips drew everyone's glance to the last occupant at the table. A large emerald glinted on one of the impatient digits. Everything about this gentleman was precise, no injudicious tugging had displaced a single hair of his close-cropped Caesar cut, his short sideburns framed his high, prominent cheekbones, and a thin patrician nose led the way to a pair of very thin lips whose natural expression seemed to be a sneer. A matching emerald tiepin nestled in the folds of his meticulously starched cravat, its glitter reflected in the cold green eyes that stared resentfully across at the earl.

"It wants three o'clock yet, Atherton," he drawled, not quite able to keep the bitterness from his voice. "I for one would like the chance to recoup some of my losses."

"Ah, Rutley," the earl sighed, "loath though I am to disappoint, I really have had enough you know."

A cynical smile twisted those thin lips. "Enough of winning?"

Hard grey eyes clashed with agate green. "Enough of everything, my dear fellow, your revenge must wait for another occasion." The voice remained soft, but the implacable note was unmistakeable and offering only the briefest of bows, the earl turned and left the room.

It was this strange humour that had persuaded him to try the new discreet hell on King

Street. He wasn't in the mood to parry the usually pointless banter with which his cronies at Whites would have no doubt regaled him. His own unexpected succession to his late father's honours, had recently made him the butt of a wide range of singularly foolish marriage mart jests. Thank God his mourning status excused him from attending all the great squeezes of the season where he might be expected to do the pretty for the latest round of insipid debutantes.

Sir Philip accompanied his friend along Old Bond Street in companionable silence for a time, somewhat doubtful that Atherton was even aware of his presence so distracted did he seem. Only the odd hackney or the call of the night watchmen claiming a fine night and the advanced hour broke the silence.

"You've made an enemy of Rutley if I'm not much mistaken," he finally ventured.

Lord Atherton seemed to turn this thought over in his mind for a moment before shrugging somewhat fatalistically. "What, after all, can he do to me, Philip?"

Sir Philip's normally cheerful mien had temporarily deserted him, a slight frown lurked at the back of his usually smiling eyes. "Nothing, I should imagine," he conceded. "But I hear he's been playing deep and losing more often than not. There's talk that nothing but an heiress will keep his creditors from his door."

This depressing news seemed of little interest to Lord Atherton. "So he's likely to be the latest is he? I fail to see, however, what the devil that has to do with me."

A short laugh escaped his friend. "You're a damned cool fish tonight, George. It has, of course, nothing to do with you. But he had an ugly, almost desperate look about him and if looks were pistols, you'd have had a bullet through your brain tonight."

Atherton gave a rather harsh laugh. "At least that would save me from the prospective lists of suitable wives my well-meaning but annoyingly persistent sisters have already drawn up for me."

"I sympathise, dear chap, and whilst I acknowledge it to be tiresome to be seen as a fish to be caught on someone's none-too-subtle lure, I hardly think death preferable."

"I apologise, Philip. I am less than good company tonight. Have none of this season's beauties caught your eye yet?"

Sir Philip smiled. "Oh my eye, yes, but it is all so tame, so dull. None of them have any spirit. I'd rather have someone challenge me than smile charmingly and agree with everything I say." He suddenly laughed at himself.

"You are making me as maudlin as you, dear fellow, it won't do."

At the point where Davies St met Grosvenor St, the friends parted. Lord Atherton carried on towards Grosvenor Square whilst Sir Philip proceeded towards Brook St. His friend's unusual mood preoccupied him so he didn't notice a dark figure, no more than a shadow, dart back into Brook Mews. However, this slight wraith had no interest other than to remain unseen and waited patiently until he had passed before continuing furtively towards the dark, winding Avery Row where a modest cart and horse awaited.

"Come on, miss, best away whilst this blindman's holiday lasts!"

The lithe figure climbed aboard and let out a low chuckle. "Stop fretting, Ned, all's well," she assured him.

A disapproving grunt was the only answer she received. Her reluctant escort showed an unerring knowledge of London as he led her down the less frequented alleys past Bloomsbury and into Holborn. It was not long before they pulled into the back entrance of Prowett's Coffee House on Red Lion Street, which any slightly impoverished gentleman could tell you served up an excellent ordinary but had no idea that a lady of undoubted quality was, at present, living upstairs.

Her room faced onto the street and a sudden shout of laughter drew her to her window. Drawing the curtain slightly to one side, she glanced outside. The street lamps threw just enough light for her to make out two entwined figures in the doorway opposite. A young man had his face buried in the ample bosom of his chosen companion for the evening. She saw the painted older lady draw back for an instant, her hand outstretched for payment before she allowed him to continue in his amorous pursuits. She sighed and let the curtain drop back into place. She only hoped that the poor unfortunate soul that was forced to tolerate the attentions of the young buck pawing her, was getting well paid for her services. It was a sight she had seen only too often since making her temporary home here to be shocked. It might have been expected that a lady of quality would have taken out her venom on the fallen woman but she had seen enough since her brief sojourn in town to realise that poverty was rife, and the women often didn't have a choice, whereas it seemed the young men had nothing to think of but their own pleasures. How she despised them. They were the privileged ones who were in a position of power and could, if they would, make some sort of difference to the world. But instead they used their wealth to further their own trivial pleasures, be it through gambling, drinking or whoring.

Reaching into her coat, she withdrew a slim case and dropped it onto the desk, before seating herself and pulling open one of the drawers. She retrieved a rather crumpled document and allowed a grim smile to curl her unfashionably full lips as she crossed out yet another name on her list. Lord Rutley would wake up tomorrow morning to find himself the latest victim of the Mayfair Thief. She regarded the closed case for a moment before opening it, the famous Rutley emeralds twinkled forgivingly in the light of the two candles that lit her small desk. Of course, the theft may have remained undiscovered for some time if she hadn't left her calling card. That would not have suited her purposes at all, especially if the latest rumours going around the coffee room downstairs that he was so badly dipped he was going to pay his addresses to the heiress of a prominent merchant in the city, young enough to be his daughter, were true. She was surprised he hadn't already sold them. That was after all, what her father had done with all but a few of her mother's treasures and those she had been forced to sell at a fraction of their worth to fund her present frugal existence. A tentative knocking on the door recalled her attention to the present.

"Come in, Lucy," she called softly, quickly adding the correct label to tonight's haul. It wouldn't do to get them mixed up, she did after all intend to return every item she had successfully stolen, eventually.

"Oh, look at you, Rosie," her old nurse scolded, grabbing the cloth that hung from the washstand. "Here, let me get that muck off you."

Rosalind submitted meekly to the rigorous scrubbing required to remove the soot from her face.

"Why can't you wear a loo mask instead? You'll be ruining that lovely complexion of yours if you're not careful. Where's all this going to end? That's what I want to know," Lucy grumbled. "You'll end up in Newgate and no mistake if you don't give up this lark soon."

Rosalind smiled fondly down at the plump, anxious face of her most faithful servant and friend, wondering which of the two hazards was bothering her old nurse more.

"Well I don't happen to have a loo mask at present but I admit it's not a bad idea," she conceded graciously, "but it will take more than a half-asleep watchman armed with a lantern and a stick or a couple of foxed gentlemen to catch me, Lucy, never fear."

Lucy took a step back and planted her small, capable hands on her wide hips. "Of course there's no danger at all, that's why you won't even take my Ned in with you."

Rosalind's smile faded. "He helps me enough as it is. I may not think the risk that great, but you know I won't put anyone else in danger. This is my game and I'll play it out."

Recognising the finality in her charge's clipped tones, Lucy sighed long and deep.

"Well, let's get you out of those clothes, my girl, they're positively indecent."

With no more ado she stripped the clinging breeches and dark, close-fitting coat from Rosalind's tall, willowy form, threw a nightgown over her head, cursorily dragged a brush through her raven locks and tucked her up in bed, her rough, disapproving attentions in no way concealing her very real affection.

Rosalind stretched limbs suddenly weary and offered a tired smile. "It's nearly over, only one left on my list."

Lucy paused in the act of packing away the items of clothing that had so offended her sensibilities. "Well, and what then, missy? What's to become of you when you won't even sell your haul? You may as well benefit from those as has stolen your inheritance from you."

"Go to bed, Lucy, you have to be up again in a couple of hours," Rosalind murmured, even as sleep dragged her down into its clinging embrace.

Tonight the dreams came thick and fast. She was back at her childhood home, Roehaven Manor; her father had been drinking again and instead of showing his only child his usual careless affection he had locked her in her room. Confused and resentful, she had rebelled. Always a tomboy and excellent at climbing, she had thought nothing of opening her window and clambering onto the nearest branch of the tree outside, from where it was an easy descent to the garden.

Like a moth to a flame, she had been drawn to the lights in her father's study window. There she had found the reason for her incarceration, around a small table by the fire sat her father and three gentlemen, none of whom she recognised not having benefited from a season in London. So engrossed were they in the turn of the cards she was in little danger of being seen. A hard anger had settled within her as she had studied her father's red, prematurely lined face, his thick brows drawn together in a fierce frown of concentration. She noticed his hand was slightly unsteady as he picked up the glass beside him and drained it.

He had taken to hard drinking and gambling after her mother's death five years previously and she knew from the drastic reduction in staff at the manor that it was only a matter of time before they lost their home. As Willow, their long-suffering butler, entered the room carrying another bottle of burgundy, she ducked beneath the stone lintel but not before she was sure he had seen her. A trusted friend, he did not give her away and she turned and ran in the moonlight through the increasingly wild gardens.

Her dream shifted and she was standing beside her father, gripping his hand tightly as she looked on her beautiful mother's pale, still face. Although she knew she was dead from the dreadful bout of influenza she had suffered, she still silently willed her to open those soft, gentle brown eyes.

Next, she was back in her bedroom, huddled under the covers, as they could no longer afford to have the fires going as a matter of course, when a loud shot shattered the night, causing her to shoot upright.

"Hush now, it's alright my love, Lucy's here," came a soothing voice.

Rosalind forced heavy eyes open to find her shaking body clasped closely to her old nurse's bosom. Relaxing into the warm embrace, she allowed silent tears to fall. When this was all over, when all of the fine gentlemen who had bled her father dry had been punished in some small way, she hoped the dreams would stop.

Printed in Great Britain
by Amazon

21249841R00071